BEGINNERS LUCK

BEGINNERS LUCK

EMILY HAHN

ISBN: 978-93-5420-296-4

Published: -

LECTOR HOUSE LLP
E-MAIL: lectorpublishing@gmail.com

BEGINNERS LUCK

BY

EMILY HAHN

OTHER WORKS:
SEDUCTIO AD ABSURDUM

TO
MITCHELL DAWSON

CONTENTS

CHAPTER ONE

He stepped off the train at Lamy expecting nothing at all. He had no idea of the city he was entering: what it looked like, how one passed the time, what people one would know — it was all unexplored. He had never in his life been west of Buffalo. Mary, his mother, had written him a few letters about it, but she had not had time to write much, and anyway she was very busy finding out for herself. Mary expected to settle down in Santa Fé for a long time; it was good for her health out here and she liked it.

Blake, on the other hand, had no plans. He was not supposed to have any: he was too young to have plans. Mary had plans for him, no doubt, but as yet he had no notice of them.

He stood for two forlorn minutes on the platform at Lamy, wondering what to do next. A chauffeur — a stranger — found him and took him in hand and put him away, with the baggage, in a new limousine. The limousine then turned around and began to drive up a winding hill, toward Santa Fé, Mary and revelation.

It was a beautiful drive up a long hill, the road twisting and leading up and down in an intriguing manner. Blake tried hard to appreciate it, but his mind would not behave. It kept reverting to another theme; a tiresome theme; a threadbare theme. His mind was an independent disagreeable thing with a passion for theatrical revivals. Just now it disregarded the beautiful heights of the Sangre de Cristo mountains and devoted itself to a New England scene, the setting of an unpleasant memory. Heedless of Blake's desire, it carried the props to the stage and set them up. Wearily, Blake helped. Obediently he placed the head-master's desk in the exact middle of the head-master's room, just below the window that looked out on the front view of the school. Doggedly he put the head-master into the chair behind the desk, and sullenly took up his own old position before the desk, facing Dr. Miller. Everything was ready, and with lifted hand Dr. Miller began the dialogue:

DR. MILLER: I regret the necessity of this more than you can possibly realize, Lennard. Some day, I hope that you will remember this moment and then perhaps you will understand the difficulty of my position. This is a moment that I have been dreading, frankly, dreading for some months.

BLAKE: I'm very sorry, sir.

DR. MILLER: It is a little late to be sorry. You must understand it is too late. No amount of apology — —

BLAKE: I wasn't apologizing, sir. I said I was sorry. I haven't apologized.

Dr. Miller: Very well, Lennard. I have written to your mother. I hope she will understand that I have done my best. You will leave here in the morning in time to catch the nine-thirty. Your mother telegraphed that you are to go— —

Blake: I know. She telegraphed me.

Dr. Miller: I think that is all. Good-bye, Blake.

Blake: Good-bye, sir.

Dr. Miller: Once more, Lennard; I'm more sorry than I can say that this happened.

Blake: Yes, sir, good-bye, sir.

Here, at the exit, his mind was most tiresome of all. Just here at the original performance Blake had slipped while making his exit. He had done his best to leave that part out of the repetitions, but the more he struggled the more ridiculous became the by-play. Today the stumble was worse than it had ever been: he slipped on the rug at the door, waved wildly about as he tried to catch his balance, and ultimately, after the most ludicrous contortions, landed on his neck in a Charles Chaplin abandon. All of this went on just as the limousine turned from the Lamy cut-off to the main road. Writhing in an agony of embarrassment, Blake forgot where he was and said aloud, in protest to the tyrannical stage-manager, "No, I didn't!"

The chauffeur cocked an ear and Blake burrowed down hastily behind a suitcase. He left the charade with relief and began to look at the mountains. Up ahead there was a group of buildings that looked as if it might be the outpost of Santa Fé. It occurred to him that he might ask the chauffeur to point things out to him. On second thought he decided to wait and pick up his knowledge in a different way. The effort of breaking silence would be terrific.

So in silence they rode down the hill into town, past the first little adobe houses and then by way of the outskirts to his mother's house. He liked the outside of it: irregular and old-looking, with a wall that started at the side and enclosed—imperfectly—a garden. Mary heard the car and came to the door, in quite a hurry. That was nice of her and it made Blake feel better. He had expected to find the door locked.

She kissed him and didn't mention school. She asked after his aunt in New York, disapproved of his tie, and sent him to his room to get acquainted. There were three pieces of furniture in it: a low bed with straight brown posts, a light dressing-table, and a wardrobe. The walls were painted a light yellow and he walked all the way around wondering how to decorate them with murals. He would need a bookcase: he could paint it himself, purple to match the mountains. But now as he looked from the window the mountains were not purple. They were blue, a deep expressionless color. They were like pieces of passe-partout about the edge of the valley, cut out in great rolling curves and pasted over the disorderly meeting of sky and land. He leaned out of the window and sniffed. His nose expected an odor of pine and wet ground; instead there was a faint parched perfume of burning wood and sunburnt clay. It was almost dark. He changed his tie and went in to tea.

Bob Stuart had come to welcome him. Sitting on the edge of a chair, talking fast and gesticulating with his free hand while he steadied his tea-cup on his knee, he looked all wrong out here. He was practically an uncle and he belonged to another world. He was embarrassing to Blake; he took from the adventure and the new world its exclusive adventurous quality. Still, he had changed. A funny little man with all his ideas coming in rushes, bubbling over in sudden gestures and rapid words, his orange hair had gained a dignity and he was not just an amusing little person. He was unique. After forty-some years of managing to hold his own, Bob had become independent. It was as if he had waked one day and stood in front of the mirror, probably with his stiff hair leaning the wrong way and his nose comically pink and small above the striped pajamas. Perhaps he had suddenly said to himself:

"Well, that's the way I am. What are they going to do about it? I am I. That's that."

It must have been something like that. At any rate, immediately thereafter other people saw a change in Bob. He had put on a velvet shirt of vivid purple, white Mexican trousers, and brown sandals that exposed his big toes to friends and enemies, and to hell with them. He walked the streets of Santa Fé with his nose up, neither seeking nor shunning mirrors. It was not at all the same old Bob who now shook hands with Blake.

"Well, well, well," he said as the hands went up and down. "And how's the young rebel?"

This was a difficult question. Blake simpered and forgot to say anything. Bob made a benevolent groaning noise and patted him on the shoulder.

"You'll outgrow it; you'll outgrow it. Here, I have another young rebel for you to meet. Teddy! Where has he gone?"

"Huh?" Over in the corner some one was prowling about looking at the pictures. He came out of the shadows and stood waiting.

"This is Teddy Madden. He ran away from home and came here to find himself and be a genius." Bob patted Teddy now, in the same fashion. "You must be great friends. Teddy, this boy has just been expelled from school. He's going to tell us why."

Across the painful benevolence that trembled in the air, the boys looked at each other and took stock. Madden was older. His legs and arms were sure of themselves. But he was not quite grown up; his mouth was not quite sure.

"Teddy's a great artist," Bob said. "Artists always run away from home, Mary. It's a law of Nature. Didn't they tell you that at school?" he asked Blake.

"No, sir. They never talk about artists at all."

"Oh, come now." Bob leaned forward hopefully, with his tirade against modern education all ready in his mouth. "Do you mean to say that you didn't study Michelangelo?"

"But that's not art," Blake said, in all sincerity. "That's Ancient History."

"And that's an epigram, my son," said Mary.

Madden seemed pleased. "Whether it is or not, it's a good one," he said. Very sure of himself, he stood by Mary and handed tea-cups around.

Of all of them the tea-pot seemed to be the only one that expected anything of the gathering. The others subsided and waited for the tea-pot to make a remark that would start things going. Blake looked at it almost hopefully, it was so authoritative. What would it say? Being a member of the family, it had a good deal of license. Being of an aristocratic and expensive shape, it would doubtless waive its right, like Mary, and remain as composed and silent as Mary herself. This is just what it did.

Under his own half-developed sense of responsibility Blake squirmed. It was all his fault. If he had not been here, the tea party would have been an informal pleasant thing. If he had been in his own room studying Latin or looking out of the window at the reluctant New England spring, Mary and Bob would even now be talking smoothly, worrying about nothing at all. If he had not been here, gripping his cup with an angry defiance, Teddy Madden would have been free to go back into the corner and read. Instead, here they all sat, looking at each other.

Bob cleared his throat and said loudly, "Well, Blake, what was it all about? Tell us what crime you committed. We're waiting."

Mary looked distressed, but said nothing.

"I guess Dr. Miller wrote as much as I could tell you," said Blake.

"He wrote, of course, darling," said Mary. "He has a way of obscuring things. We just couldn't make it out at all."

"He writes an extraordinary letter," added Bob. "Extraordinary. Wasn't it, Ted?"

"Absolutely," said Madden. Blake was suddenly furious that Madden had seen it. What business was it of Madden's? What had his mother been thinking of?

There were little pin-scratches on the wood of his chair. Some of them formed designs; just next to his hand on the right chair-arm was a lopsided fleur-de-lys. But the design in the cloth of his trousers was different; eyed closely, it had the appearance of a family of brown triangles turning their backs with one accord on another family of tan triangles....

"Blake," said Mary gently.

He answered, "Well, I'm just trying to think of what to say. I don't know what the matter is. I can't get along with people, I guess."

"What sort of people, darling?"

"Any sort. Masters. Boys. Anybody. It's my general attitude."

"What?" cried Bob, smiling.

"My general attitude. That's what Dr. Miller said. He said I was unsocial and spoiled and an irritant to the community."

"Yes, yes, yes," said Bob. "But what did you *do*? He wouldn't have sent you away for that. There must have been something more specific."

"There wasn't, really. I had a row with the English master about a theme because I left out some commas and they were putting it into the school magazine and he edited it. He put the commas back in and ran some of the sentences together so that they would be well-rounded, he said. I told him he hadn't any right to do it. He didn't have, either. He said there were certain rules of language, and I said, all right, I would make up some more. He was sore."

"What else?" said Mary.

"Then there were lots of little things. Mother, I hate that place. I told you, Christmas. I said this would happen."

"But you promised to try, dear. Did you?"

"I did try at first. There was a meeting in the auditorium last week and there was a man there to talk. He used to be a friend of Roosevelt and he was Miller's cousin. They always play the Star Spangled Banner and you're supposed to stand at attention, and I didn't."

"But why didn't you?" said Bob. Blake said nothing. He couldn't explain. It had been a sudden rush of anger at everything; he couldn't put that feeling into words for Bob.

"Well, dear, and then?"

"I was called up to Miller and we had a fight about everything that had happened. There was something else; a silly old fight about making too much noise in the library."

Blake's eyes met Teddy's, and he thought he saw the other boy nod at him. He was a little comforted.

"Well, well, well," said Bob, standing up, "it's a revolutionary age. We mustn't take these things too seriously, Mary. Remember, we all outgrow it. I must be getting along. Come on, Ted. Remember Tuesday."

He patted Blake's head, kissed Mary, and went out. Teddy nodded casually and followed him. He looked a little embarrassed.

Mary patted Blake's head, too, but she couldn't think of anything to say. He put down a cookie on the table and said, "I'm awfully sorry. I couldn't help it, honestly."

"I know. But I'm a little worried. What will you do in the fall?"

"Couldn't I stop trying to go to school? It's no use, really. Let me go to work."

"Don't be ridiculous, dear. What could you do?"

"I don't know. Something. I don't want to worry you."

"You know you don't worry me. I want you to find yourself."

"Uh-huh." He twirled a button on his coat.

"Well," she said, "we'll think about it. You spend the summer here and get a good rest."

"What's it like?"

"Oh, I think you'll like it very much. There are plenty of people for you to play with."

"How are you?"

"Better, I think. Doctor Browning says to be very quiet this summer, and it ought to work wonders."

"Who's Madden?"

"That's a very nice boy. Bob says he is really talented. He's been here since early spring; I think he worked his way out just so he could join the art colony. So many of those boys do that sort of thing.... I think that we might find another school for you, dear, or a tutor. It would mean only one more year, and you'll like college."

"No, I won't. I don't want to go. Please."

"Well, we'll see.... I think dinner is ready."

He almost fell asleep at the table. It was the fault of the fire, so near his chair. He couldn't stop watching it. Along the cracks in the charcoal, little blue flames walked up and down lapping at the air. The room was filled with the faint parched sweet smell.

Anxious to get to his room and to look again at the mountains, he kissed Mary and went to bed. He undressed and lay down and turned to the window. But now there was nothing but darkness; the sky was full of very big bright stars and around the edge of the world there were no more stars. Big shadows had blotted them out, but what shape the shadows had or how far away they were, it was impossible to say. He drew his knees up and rubbed the pillow with his cheek and closed his eyes.

For a long time he could not go to sleep; he kept his eyes shut with an effort, against the waiting mass of the mountains; he smiled and jerked his pillow closer to his shoulder, with a nervous alert hand.

CHAPTER TWO

"And over there is Camel Rock," Gin shouted, trying to reach the far corners of the bus with her voice. Just then the driver went into low and made it more difficult. She sat as near the edge of her seat as she could without falling off when the bus turned a corner and rocked a bit. Eleven heads turned obediently towards Camel Rock.

"See it?" she screamed. "See the hump, and the head in front?" Her voice almost cracked.

They all saw it at last. Those who couldn't at first were helped by the others, standing up to look back at it while the bus went on. Gin sat back in the seat again and relaxed, swallowing hard. There would be nothing more to show them until Santa Clara; perhaps she could be quiet until then. She looked around to see if anyone was nursing a grievance. Would they expect her to keep talking in between the points of interest? Sometimes people wanted her to, other times they preferred to sleep. There was a fat man in the third seat who showed signs of being difficult; the kind of tourist who wrote letters to the company after the trip, commending and criticizing. Every courier lived in terror of such a letter.

"While I have nothing but praise for the courtesy and attention of your driver, I am sorry to say that none of us were satisfied with Miss Arnold's behaviour. She seemed distracted; she did not attend to her duties. She seemed to lose no opportunity for disappearing from us; whenever the occasion offered itself for her to wander off, she was nowhere to be found. I am unwilling to complain about anything connected with your excellent tours, but I must say that when I have paid an extra fare of forty-seven dollars and fifty cents...."

Gin took a deep breath and leaned forward to the fat man.

"Do you like this road, Mr. Butts?" she asked tenderly. "It's quite famous. The guests always like it. I do think that this is one of the nicest trips we have, even if it *is* included in the regular Detour. The first and third days may be more educational, but today I think you'll have a lovely time besides."

Mr. Butts merely grunted, but there was a satisfactory reaction from the old lady who sat in front of him. She turned and smiled nervously.

"Isn't this road dangerous for the speed we're going?" she quavered. "Of course it's perfectly beautiful. Mr. Butts, do look at that, right behind you!"

Mr. Butts turned his head resignedly and looked. The bus had come to a place that gave a short glimpse of Santa Fé behind them, tiny and white and scattered. It was immediately hidden by the dark turbulent waves of hill around it as they drove on.

"Pretty," said Mr. Butts in his brief way.

Gin gave it up for the moment and settled back, fanning herself with her hat. The bus was hot and stuffy, although all the glass windows were open. She yawned and drifted off, thankful that she wasn't feeling particularly nauseated today by the constant motion. Some of the girls could never get used to it, but she seemed to be adjusted. She looked around apathetically at the dudes and wondered if they were all as stupid as they appeared or if it was because she needed sleep. Some days, it was true, everyone was perfectly charming. Those were the days that followed good healthy nights of sleep. There weren't many of them, she thought ruefully. She often thought ruefully of her habits, but never to the extent of changing them. No one did in Santa Fé when they had lived there as long as she had.

One of the crowd today wasn't so bad, she thought. She had noticed him at the hotel office when he signed on at the last minute for the trip. As skilful as the clerk in sizing up the tourists, she had put him immediately in the pigeon-hole reserved for summer visitors who stayed the season. He was no train-tripper. He probably lived in one of the big houses outside of town, with a swimming-pool and a stable. A nice-looking kid, just a baby, probably sixteen. Since she had not seen him before, he must be new. Since he was wearing summer clothes of an extreme carelessness—blue shirt and white trousers and no hat—he was not a resident; residents of Santa Fé never admitted that it was a summer resort; they tried to dress as if Santa Fé were New York. Well, he'd be around now, riding around the Plaza, playing tennis with Teddy Madden, looking scornfully at the newcomers after he had been there a week, and talking learnedly of Indian customs. He was new, though: she could tell it by the fact that he was taking a trip with her and looking at everything with an ingenuous pleasure. She liked the way he looked out of the window. He was taking it hard.

It made her pensive and reminiscent: his youthful rapt gaze. She thought of the first time she had driven out here, with the couriers' training school. It had been raining; up on Baldy there was a light snow and there was mist around Jemez. She had felt terribly excited. All the other girls told her it was the altitude. Whatever it was, she liked it. And then the bus had come near Española and the valley.... They were almost there now; she watched the boy like a cat, to see what would happen to him when he saw it.

Yes, he got it. She knew it by the way his thin little shoulders jerked and his head leaned back, closer to the window. She could just see the back of his head, but she knew. When *she* had first seen it, she had cried. Probably the effect of the altitude, but why not? There was nothing like it anywhere else. The valley was absolutely naked; bare rock shaped in lumps on the bare sand, drowning in mists of vague lavender and dark blue and thin brown and yellow, transparent colors. The rock was shaped in pillars and blocks and squat cylinders, cut off flat at the tops. It was all dead and ghostly. Nothing lived here. The few scraggy clumps of juniper were not alive, for they were as ancient and dusty as the rocks, and as motionless.

It was only for a few miles. Beyond, the land lived again, flushed to foliage by the lazy sandy river. Back of all of it were the real mountains, with pine forests and trout streams, but now while Gin and the boy looked at them they were too far off to be green; they were dead dark blue.

"My, that's gloomy," said the cheerful lady from Chicago. "Miss Arnold, is that land good for anything? Does the government own it, or what?"

They crossed the wide white bridge to Española and followed the road through a rocky country, bearing down on the ugly round buildings that housed the Government schools. Approaching Santa Clara, the driver honked his horn loudly to warn the pottery-venders. By the time he came to a stop before the church, in the dry yellow plaza surrounded by square adobe huts, the women were filing out to the clear space in the centre, carrying their pottery on their heads and swinging baskets of smaller stuff—modelled animals, black-painted, and bead belts and necklaces. They walked serene and fat, surrounded by children and yellow dogs. They sat down in a neat half-circle before the bus and spread their wares out, impassive or smiling in their cotton shawls and long smocks. Eleven potential customers climbed out of the leather chairs and looked curiously at the big black bowls and the brown faces.

The men of the party were already saying, "That would be fine for Cousin Sally," and the women were saying, "Now, John, be careful. We've just packed the trunk as it is; we can't buy everything we see," when Gin slipped away. She hurried around the corner of a house and walked down one of the many back paths, trying to get away before someone asked her to argue with an Indian about the price of the bowls. She stopped at one of the screen doors and peeped in. Her friend was at home, making a bowl in the middle of the whitewashed clay floor.

"Oh, come in, Ginny," said Rufina, pushing a chair with her feet. "I heard you coming. How are you? I haven't seen you here for a week. Been sick?"

"No, they sent me to the Canyon all of a sudden, and I just got back yesterday. How's all the family?" A sticky little girl, pursued by flies, climbed up in her lap.

"Not so good. My mother is still sick, but she is getting better. Did you bring many people today?"

"One full load, that's all."

"We have been busy. Yesterday there were so many. Two buses and other people coming by themselves, all day."

Outside the door a bulky shadow fell. It was the lady from Chicago, reconnoitering on her own. Gin wondered if she had been walking into any of the houses without knocking; it sometimes had an oddly infuriating effect on the Indians.

"Oh, there's Miss Arnold right at home in the middle of them. Come here, Eddie, here's the cutest thing. I want you to take a picture of it. Look, here's an Indian making a pot right in her own house. Isn't that darling? Would you think that you were in the States?"

"Come in," said Rufina. They stepped over the threshold and she sat back on her heels, smiling blankly.

"Oh, look," said the lady loudly. "A baby too, right in Miss Arnold's lap. Perfectly adorable. Miss Arnold," she asked, whispering in a small shout, "aren't you afraid of catching things? Her hair...."

Gin said that it was time to go back to the bus. She held open the door, waved good-bye to Rufina hastily, and went back to the marketplace. Eight of the dudes were back in the car, and Blake was waiting for her with a new purchase to show her, a turquoise ring.

"Let's see it," she said, and he took it off and handed it over.

"Why, it's quite nice," she said. "Did you buy it here?"

"Yes, that man over there was wearing it and I asked him if he wanted to sell. Is it really good? I liked the colour of the stone."

"The green stones always look nice, I think," she said. "Nice and old. They're not the best, of course," she added in low tones. "You probably paid more than he expected, but it's good-looking, I think."

It was not ethical to tell any dude that he had paid too much, but he didn't seem to care. He liked the ring, that was all. Summer people always collected jewelry in a serious way—they liked to have heavy bracelets sitting around on the tables or shelves in a careless, opulent manner. The old timers scorned it.

Now the other ten were sitting in the bus, and on Mr. Butts' face was a look that meant, "Must we wait all day while that hussy flirts?"

She took her own seat, thinking that she would get Mr. Butts yet.

They were growing a little impatient about lunch, she thought. The long drive up to Puye, around a hairpin turn that made the Chicago lady squeal for three minutes, distracted them a little from the idea of food. But not much. On top of the plateau while they were exclaiming over the view she thought of something that might get the wedge into Mr. Butts.

"In November," she said as they entered the forest, "there are wild turkeys here. Lots of the boys in town shoot a couple during the season." He grunted, but turned to look again at the neat wooded lawns. "He's slipping," she thought hopefully.

The cliffs of Puye were nearer: pale yellow in the pale brightness of the air. Higher and higher they went, round big curves that pulled them closer to the caves with every sweep. She showed them the caves——

"See those dark spots? Those are the cliff-dwellings we came out to see. Yes, we'll see them much closer than this, Mrs. Jennings. We're going to climb right up; right up there." Mrs. Jennings squealed a little. She had them already, Gin reflected; she had all of them but Mr. Butts. How long would he take?

They swarmed over the rest-house when the bus came to a halt.

"Lunch!" she cried gaily. Mr. Butts seemed unimpressed. The hostess called her into the kitchen and whispered, "I'm at my wits' ends. Will you please put it into your report again tonight? I simply cannot manage without another maid.

I'm sorry, Gin, but I don't think you'll have much time for your own lunch today. Would you mind eating it afterwards?"

Gin carried plates and glasses back and forth from the kitchen to the living-room. Mrs. Jennings offered to help in a very sportsmanslike Western manner, but she was refused. Gin was horrified at the idea of a dude stepping into the kitchen. The hostess worked furiously unpacking the lunch that had come on the back of the bus; jellied soup and salad and apricot pie.

"Gosh, I get sick of this soup," said Gin disconsolately in the kitchen, talking to the cook. "It's worse when I have three trips to the same place in succession. Some day I'll start bringing my own lunch." She walked over to the window and watched the dudes disporting on the porch, fully fed and happy, teasing the rest-house puppy. Mr. Butts looked dour, however. He hadn't been able to eat the apricot pie or the sandwiches because he was on a diet. "That fat one," she told the cook, "is pretty bad."

The cook looked over her shoulder and agreed heartily. "They all travel, that kind. Nobody will keep them at home. Have some more coffee?"

"No thanks. We'll have to be starting. Well...." With a gesture of tightening her belt, she walked out to the porch. "Well, people, are we ready to go?"

"Where to?" asked Mr. Butts.

"Right up there." She pointed to the stone-stepped hill behind the house, with the caves at the top of a long climb. Mr. Butts seemed to hesitate. "Curly's going," Gin added, nodding to the driver. "Aren't you, Curly?"

"Sure thing. I'll take care of you."

Mrs. Jennings was the first to step forward. "All right; if Curly can make it, I can."

Mr. Butts' masculinity conquered, and he set out without further discussion. Blake had evidently gone on ahead; they could see him at the top with his hands in his pockets, looking around in a very pleased fashion all by himself.

There is a steep ladder at the top of the hill which leads from the slope to the flat summit. It sometimes causes a lot of trouble to people who have not caught their breath while they study the caves. Two of the ladies in Gin's party looked at it fearfully and refused to climb it at all. They proposed to go down again to the rest-house, and said that they were satisfied with what they had seen. This feminine timidity spurred Mr. Butts to a genial teasing attitude. He laughed at the ladies; he taunted them; he essayed the ladder and found it easily conquered. From the top he persuaded them to be brave and come along. With pushing, pulling, lifting and pleading, they all managed to get there, and they gathered in a triumphant panting group about Gin, talking of mountain climbing in Switzerland and taking pictures of the ladder. She gathered her flock about her on the wind-swept summit and lectured on the glory that was Puye, waving to the piles of debris that once were houses and pointing out the dry water-hole. They walked the length of the village and peered into the excavations. They looked down upon the distant top of the rest-house. They stood up straight and breathed hard and gazed for miles over the tree-tops to the distant mountains, which did not look so high as they had before. Blake sauntered away and looked for bits of pottery. And Gin kept a wary eye on the red face of Mr. Butts.

"Yes, he's slipping," she told herself.

Afterwards they started home, a long silent ride that was uninterrupted except for a short visit to Tesuque. They were too tired to take much interest in Tesuque, which after all was just another Indian village. Of course, there was old Teofilo. Teofilo was a great help with his professional attitude of glad-hander; he greeted all couriers with the same glad surprise, although he saw at least one a day, and he was more than willing to show his scarred head, which had once been scalped. He loved to have his picture taken.

Then, the rest of the way was quiet. The dudes arranged their cameras in their laps, peered around at the bigger pots stored in the back of the bus, and settled down to doze. The afternoon waned and the shadows lengthened across the road and the mountains darkened. In town, Curly manipulated the bus through the narrow streets and stopped before the Palace of the Governors, now a museum.

"We stop here to see the Museum," Gin shouted through the bus. "Indian relics and paintings and the chair Lew Wallace wrote 'Ben Hur' in. Afterwards we walk back to the hotel."

"Good-bye," said Blake suddenly, and climbed out. Off across the Plaza he sprinted; he could be seen intercepting Teddy Madden just as he was going into the drug store. Gin looked after them and wondered if Teddy had made any attempt to call her that morning. Perhaps she had better call him and remind him that they had a date. He was so forgetful. Mechanically she ushered the dudes into the Palace, then to the first room on the right.

"Now, here we have a model of the place we saw yesterday. See, here's the ruined church...."

But if she called Teddy, Harvey would answer the phone and might think that she had called to speak to him. Had she a good enough excuse for calling Teddy? Was she justified in assuming that they were good enough friends? Oh, to hell with that. There was no reason why she shouldn't call him.

"This is the Frijoles room. Frijoles is one of the places we have for private tours. It is very lovely and very famous: it's all excavated. We take it in one-day trips or two: there's a hotel with cabins for rooms. It's most interesting. It has cave-dwellings similar to what we saw today, but they're in the walls of the canyon instead of being on a cliff. There's a little model of the kiva; see, like the ceremonial cave we saw today."

With a guilty feeling, she came back to the business in hand and listened to herself talking like a Victrola. That was no way to act. One must put oneself over. Mr. Butts was looking at the pictures on the walls with a thoughtful eye, a competitive eye. She smiled at him, glowing with all the force of her personality.

"I'll tell you what effect that has on me, Mr. Butts," she said confidentially. "When I stand there in that canyon I get the queerest feeling." It was true, that was the worst of all, she thought. The idea of telling him! "When I'm there I can't help feeling that the people who used to live in those caves are still there, in a way. They're being very quiet, and looking at me." She paused and stared at him with wide eyes. "It's silly of me, isn't it?"

Yes, she had him. He looked down at her and thought about Frijoles and the dead cave-dwellers, and he looked at her again and thought of the lost ages when men were men, and of the ladder he had climbed today, and of the letter he could write home about it. She knew it. She had him.

"You do?" he asked, and there was actually a kindly glint in that fishy eye. "So that's how it makes you feel, does it?"

He rubbed his chin. He looked at her and saw her as a person instead of a courier, a person who had watched him climb that ladder. There would be no letter to the company. She had him.

"Well, well, well," he said jovially. "Well well well."

CHAPTER THREE

The Madden boy was worried about his laundry. It was a week late, he couldn't remember who was doing it for him, and besides he was having one of those moods that made him worry about little things. It was not so much the tragic lack of socks, he told Harvey Todd, but there were three shirts in it that belonged to Bob Stuart.

"I hate not returning people's clothes," he said. "I hate wearing them in the first place but this time I couldn't help it. It's maddening."

Harvey never rose to the heights of hysteria, and this time he was almost phlegmatic. "It'll be along," he said. "Don't forget, some of it was mine. I'll help you yell when the time comes. Jesus, I'm late." He slammed down his cup on the table, between a broken tumbler and an eggy plate, and hurried out of the door, carrying his hat.

"Canaille," said Teddy humorously. "Cochon," he added into the mirror, scowling fiercely.

"Señor?" asked a tremulous voice at the door. A little girl held out a huge bundle as he opened the screen. "Eighty-four cents," she said. "My mother says she can't find one sock. She send tomorrow."

"Oh, yes? Well, tell her I'll pay then."

"Si, señor." There was boredom and cynicism in her tone as she turned away. Teddy's eyes narrowed; he thought of challenging her, but what was there to say? He shrugged and forgot it, sitting by the table and looking vacantly at the unopened bundle. The sun crept up his leg and his kneecap began to prickle pleasantly under the linen trousers. He sat still until the bundle blurred and moved gently out of itself, projecting a phantom bundle an inch away from its own crisp outlines, hovering a little above the shining top of the table on which it had lain. He dreamed; a good picture like this, with the checkered table-cloth and the spots of sunlight.... A fly bit him savagely on the ankle and he stood up.

The picture waiting for him must be finished today or he would hate himself. Last night he should not have stopped after working up to it all day. Had he gone on, it might have been really good. Could he ever do anything really good? Why couldn't he get immersed, and forget people and money and his own fading flesh? He looked at the easel and felt that he would never see it as it should be; he almost wept from exasperation. There were so many interruptions. There was his own careless incompetence, and his eternal itching to see people and to have people love him, and there was money. Money.... A familiar panic began to rise. He seized a brush and set to work.

It wouldn't go. He moved about distractedly, trying to clean up the room. The dirty plates were piled up in the sink; he made a few dabs at them and changed his mind. He looked apathetically at the stiff spotted table-cloth and hung up a leather coat that had slipped from its nail. Then he caught a glimpse of the painting from a new angle; a real feeling of interest persuaded him to get to work again.

Another hour was coaxed out of eternity. The sun crept farther into the warm house; out in the street was a growing rush of motorcars and sometimes a clatter of hoofs; the tap in the sink dripped with a cheerful chiming splash on the tumbled china. He whistled and painted. Beginning to feel cramped, he took a short walk around the room, keeping a wary eye on the canvas as if it might take flight with his spasm of energy. It was clear again; he saw just what he wanted and perhaps he could do it. But not just now.

"Stale," he said aloud to his conscience, and his voice sounded choked and rusty in the empty room. He would do something else for awhile. Shave? The idea of putting on water to heat seemed impossible. Wait till later; plenty of water at Bob's. He leaned to the mirror and rubbed his chin thoughtfully, wondering how he would look with a beard. Bob wouldn't like it. That reminded him of the shirts and he untied the laundry, sorting it out and hesitating sometimes, sock in hand, between the two piles of segregated underwear, his own and Harvey's. He always gave himself the benefit of the hesitation. But it meant nothing: Harvey would ravage his store at the first necessity.

The work impulse was quite dead. He felt relieved, as though he had flung a small morsel into the maw of his conscience, but otherwise there was no twinge of energy. He tied up Bob's shirts and put the last unbroken record on the rickety little Victrola, borrowed one evening from Gin and still unreturned. They needed records: the Lennards had good records. Blake kept up pretty well; he probably just walked into a place and bought up everything. Pretty soft for him.

Well, one could make out by snuggling up to the big houses, riding in their cars and going to their parties and drinking their liquor. One smothered the occasional fever of hopeless malice. They couldn't help being lazy and easily pleased and careless. If only they wouldn't try to be critical about painting. There must be things they couldn't have; there must be.

"When I am rich," he thought, and then, "but if I never am?"

He paused with a clean towel in his hand, and looked around. The room was still the same, small and bare and cluttered and dirty. Outside the window was a blue mountain-peak beyond a broad dwindling stretch of juniper-dotted sand, but around his house there were other little low houses, mud houses sinking in the mud of the road. He turned slowly around, looking hopelessly at the yellow walls and at the tiny fire-place spilling pine ash out on the floor. The picture was shining wetly and tiny knobs of paint on the canvas shed tiny shadows. He frowned at it, stepped suddenly closer and examined it carefully.

The letter-box outside clanged in closing, and he heard the postman going away. More bills? Perhaps there would be something else: he decided to see. There was a letter from home, from Minnesota.

The very sight of the postmark sent a heavy lump to his chest. If he didn't open it? If he dropped it into the gray ashes by accident, and waited until Harvey had burned it in the evening? Busy with the thought, he moved his hand up and down balancing it, weighing it. To open it would mean the day lost, with all his work ruined. He would read it and then flee from the close little room, searching madly all over town for someone—anyone—who knew nothing about Minnesota or families: someone rich and lazy and lucky and dumb; some stranger. Burn it; burn the next one and the next and the next. Burn it.

With a despairing glance at his mountain, a farewell glance, he tore it open and found a check for ten dollars, blotted a little and somehow nibbled at the edges. The letter was on blue-lined paper. From the little square sheets rose an almost visible feeling, like smoke; the room was steeped in Teddy's guilt. And yet it was a nice letter.

> "Dear Teddy," his mother had written, innocently enough, at the old brown desk in the front room. "I don't want to scold you in this letter because I know it is hard to find time to write when you are getting started, I thought that I would have to tell you that your father gets worried. I tell him not to be foolish as I am sure if anything had happened we would be notified right away. He worries about everything these days because business is not very good. We are very well except for a cold that has run through the family, I hope you are taking care of yourself, I can't help thinking that you are too young to be so far away. Tommy's report from school is a little better than it has been especially on spelling. There is not much news, the Dibbles are having a hard time with Kenneth, I am afraid he is a wild boy. Tommy saw him Saturday night with that girl at the drug store and they had been drinking. I am so sorry for Mrs. Dibble, I am sure if a son of mine acted like that it would kill your father. He was saying this morning he could probably speak to Mr. Larsen about your working in the store here, I tell him it is more likely the country that is the attraction out there, the picture you sent is very pretty. Please write even a postcard, your father worries. I enclose something to help out, you don't need to mention it when you write because your father is worried about the business.
>
> Lovingly, your
> MOTHER."

The Madden boy put the letter down on the table and walked around the room, thinking. The first few minutes were always the hardest. He reasoned with himself frantically, trying to get rid of that lump in his chest. He hated himself; more than that he hated his mother. It was not right to make him feel so guilty. It was not right. People don't stay home. His father had not stayed home. He had run away to Minnesota; if he happened to marry and have children, why should they stay home?

Oh, forget it, forget it. There was the check, now. A boy in a book would send it back with interest. He couldn't do that. He couldn't just send it back like that and hurt her feelings. The only frank, honest, brave thing to do was to keep it, in the face of all families, all feelings, all outworn nests and prisons. This was his city, these his mountains. Somewhere in America there was a woman who had borne him, but everywhere there were children being born. What about it? He asked his mother that. What about it? Oh, damn.

Someone threw a rock against the door. Furiously he tore it open and looked out.

"Oh," he said, "it's you. Come in."

Blake Lennard, it was, sitting on a norse and wearing a huge Stetson. He looked light-hearted and absurd, but shy. He started to climb down.

"You're up?" he said. "No one else seems to be. I've been riding all over town trying to find my way. What I thought was that maybe you would like to ride; there is another horse up at the house. I had it saddled in case I found anyone. I want to see what it's like around here. Are you too busy?"

"Fine, no, come on in. I'll be ready in a second." The hysteria had departed. Until the next letter. Meantime there were all the playboys and the parties.

Blake stepped in, looking around with equal interest in everything, the bed with colored blankets tossed in the middle and the dusty bits of art.

"Is it yours?" he asked, looking at the picture. "I like it. Don't you? It's almost finished: weren't you working on it? Didn't I really interrupt?"

"No," said the Madden boy, crushing a piece of paper and throwing it into the fire, "I wasn't going to finish it. Chuck me that boot, will you?"

CHAPTER FOUR

Gin dropped her suitcase to the porch with a loud sigh, fished in the rusty mailbox to no avail, and fumbled with her key at the lock. The door swung open at her touch. She stared at Flo, who was garbed in the green kimono that was signal of a rest-day, and who stared back in gloomy impassivity. Her lips were puffed and her eyes were red.

"Hello!" cried Gin. "Why are you here?"

"Well, guess." Flo shuffled over to the sofa and a pile of stockings that needed darning. "I got up early this morning and went down to the office, all ready and waiting. I've been packed for two days, I was so excited."

"I know."

"Well, the cars all lined up and everybody came except three of my dudes. They were a family. I guess they just decided not to come, without any notice. It was so late that Mr. God just put the other one into Rita's car instead, and they sent her, and told me to go home. That means the third year running that I've missed out on the Hopi country."

"Oh, you poor thing!" In all Gin's rush of indignation she was afraid to say more. With her mouth open, waiting to pour forth incitement to rebellion, she looked at Flo's miserable face and turned instead to her suit-case. The purple velvet blouse went into the rickety wardrobe, but after a quick survey of the rest of the contents she closed the bag and pushed it into the corner, ready for tomorrow.

"Gee, I'm sorry," she added over her shoulder, draping her suit-coat on a hanger.

"Oh, well," said Flo heavily, "I'll be over all this by tomorrow, I suppose. I've been as sore as this before. I'm just mad because I turned down a date for tomorrow night and now I'll be in town after all, probably."

"It's a rotten deal. Call up and say your plans have changed. Where are the cigarettes?"

"On the table behind you. No, I'm not going to call up now. I'm ashamed to do it; I talked too much about the Hopi trip. I might as well give up trying to keep any contacts in this damned town. They're always being mixed up. What sort of crowd did you have?"

"Ghastly." Gin sat down on the couch and propped her feet up, taking a long comfortable puff. "It was a married couple with a kid and an old lady who kept saying, 'Now, young woman, tell me what I'm going to see!' Whenever I tried to tell her she'd look over my head with a patient expression."

"I can just see her. They come in packages." Flo picked up another stocking and spread her fingers out in the heel. "Gin, I'm fed up. Really."

"Naturally," said Gin, as comfortingly as possible.

"No, it isn't just that. I've been thinking over the whole situation. I've been here since the beginning of the Detour: I've had three years of it. Where am I? What have I got out of it?"

"What have you got?" Gin smiled and watched the smoke. "Oh, you've got a swell Navajo belt."

"Yes, a belt and a half dozen shirts I wouldn't dream of wearing if they weren't part of the uniform, and a lot of silver junk that I'm sick of looking at. I'd sell it if I didn't need it for the effect."

"But of course there's the experience. Many a girl of your age is hanging around in New York or Chicago trying to catch a husband so she can stop playing the typewriter eight hours a day. This is fun. Honestly it is: think of the city, and the dirt!"

"Experience." Flo pronounced it carefully, with a burlesque tone of rapture. "You like that word. It's the same thing as adventure, isn't it?"

"Just about."

"Yeah. I used to have ideas about adventure, too."

"Oh, you're old and weary. Forget it."

"No, I'm telling you an idea. I think that adventure isn't worth a damn unless you can talk about it afterwards. It's all in the story. I know."

"Well, go ahead and tell the story. Who's stopping you?"

"Who wants to hear it? The couriers don't want to hear about it; they have the same thing every day. I can't talk to the dudes about it. They just want to hear how many Indians are born every year."

"Or if the couriers aren't Mexican, really. Or how many stamps to use on letters to Chicago. Well, tell your friends. They enjoy it."

"What friends? I haven't any."

Gin was tired of it. "Oh, for heaven's sake, Flo. Snap out of it."

"But I haven't. Who on earth would take the trouble to go on being a friend of any of us when we're always leaving town? It takes too much energy. As soon as I make a dinner date the office deadheads me to Albuquerque to wait for some railroad official who's taking a free vacation to the canyon or something. People get tired of that. No one ever asks me for bridge any more. I never have time to write letters: I don't even feel like it. I bet a soldier gets just this way, living in training camp,... The only people I ever see in any connected way are the other girls and the drivers and the Indians. And the nigger in the lavatory on the Chief, when I'm on the trains." She broke off the thread and rolled up two stockings. "We're pathetic figures. Don't you realize it? I've been realizing it all day."

"Have it your own way," said Gin. "In my artless fashion I thought I was enjoying myself, but have it your own way. Have a drink."

"I don't care if I do."

Gin went into the kitchen, knelt down before a cabinet that was shrouded in a cretonne curtain, and pulled out a glass keg of corn liquor. She poured out two small glasses and went back to the living room.

Flo tasted hers and said again, "I'm fed up." Gin watched her curiously and felt a little depressed. Sometimes she too had a feeling of hopelessness; it was probably the same thing now with Flo. Were they coming to her more often lately? Would she too become chronically tired and aggrieved? How long before she began to indulge in that dangerous game of wondering what it was all about? She drank the corn thoughtfully, thinking about her first days here. It had all been fun, but most especially, she remembered the party the old girls had given for the new, when they had begun to tell their favorite stories about dudes. There was the girl who gave them the list of W. C.'s available for every trip, and made them practice how to ask the gentlemen if they needed them.

"You don't really need to say anything to them. You just say to the nearest woman in a loud whisper, 'Would you like to...?' and they'll watch where you go, if they have any sense."

Then there had been the last lecture, when Mr. God gave them a little talk on the aims of the company and ended his address with a delicate plea for—well, for what? Sobriety and morality, probably. What he said was, "I need hardly add that we assume that every girl is a *lady*, in the best sense of the word...."

They had giggled at that, all the way back to the apartment. It *was* fun, the whole idea; tearing over the countryside all day and not knowing every evening where you would be the next night. Flo was tired, that was all: it would pass——

"We might cut up tonight," she said aloud. "There's a new movie isn't there? Or would you like to hire a car and go out of town somewhere? Come on, let's do that."

"Don't be an idiot," Flo grumbled. "It costs too much. I don't know if I'll last till next pay day as it is. I tell you, though, we might get dressed up and eat at the hotel instead of fixing something here."

"Yes, that wouldn't be bad. Is there any hot water? Oh, wait a minute." The phone was ringing: she ran to answer it and called back, "Flo, it's Tom and he says it's going to be moonlight. He and Wally want us to go up the canyon for a picnic. Should I tell him we'll fix the supper?"

Flo frowned, as usual, and protested. "But there's nothing in the house...."

"Now, don't be that way. We can send for something. It'll do us good. Come on."

"Oh, all right. Who's going?"

"Just us and the cowboys. Tom says he can have the horses here by seven. Hurry and make up your mind, he's waiting."

"It's all right with me." She hesitated, struggling with her woe, then hurried into the kitchen and started to slice bread.

They were well on the way by the time the moon appeared over a dip in the range of hills to the east. The night air was warm; in the moonlit darkness their shadows were grotesquely different in size. Tom's hat was the largest thing about him; it swept in a beautiful curve above his sharp face. He rode ahead of the others, glancing around to talk to Flo, who followed stiff and a little ill at ease in the saddle, perpetually thinking and talking of her horse. Gin and Wally rode side by side, but Wally was immense and the horse he rode was also immense: when Gin said anything to him she had to look up. She didn't say much: Wally was in a reminiscent mood and kept the conversation going without any help.

"I mind at one of the shows at Cheyenne," he said, "the judges was just beginning to catch on the wild cow milking trick. I won out because they caught everybody else."

"What is the trick? I never heard of it."

"No, they don't do it no more. You've got to show milk in the bottle to win: the first one who gets to the stand with milk in the bottle wins the money. The boys used to carry milk right along with them, in the bottle, in their pocket, and make a few motions at the cow with it and then run along to the judges' stand. It was just a race really. This time the judges was watching out and they felt the bottles and the milk was cold so that let them out."

"And yours wasn't cold?"

"Oh no," said Wally. "I'd been carrying the milk in my mouth: it was right warm. That was the only money I took at that show."

The creaking of the saddles and the mixed beat of the horses' hoofs added to a peaceful rhythm of night noises. Passing a farmyard, a little black dog darted out with fierce yaps and Gin's horse jumped nervously and started to trot. The other three fell into the stride; gathering speed, they cantered up a rise in the road and swung around a bend into the canyon itself. A light breeze met them. Gin closed her eyes, giving herself up to the feeling. She was thinking about Teddy. It was a good thing she had managed to get out of the house tonight. She'd been spending too many evenings waiting for him to call up.

"Probably this is one of the evenings he'll decide to call," she thought, and tried to be glad that she wouldn't be there to answer the phone. "When I see him again I'll tell him I was in town, and that'll show him that I don't always wait for him." But would it do any good? Would it have any effect, and if so, what effect did she want it to have? She couldn't figure out how she felt about him. He exasperated her: she always made up her mind to quarrel with him next time she saw him—perhaps a quarrel would break down his easy, lazy indifference to everything—and then when she saw him, she always forgot. It was only when she wasn't with him that she was so exasperated. Silly to feel anything about him at all. They didn't know each other very well: they hardly ever saw each other. She wondered whether to speak to Flo about it. But Flo had no use for the Camino crowd at all: she refused to consider them human. "Nuts," she called them, and forgot all about them.

The soft ceaseless flow of words from Wally and the loping horses pushed Gin into an exaltation, after a little. She was part of the Western world at last: not the West of the daytime where people brushed their teeth and went to offices, but the real West that existed in the fifteen-cent magazines on drugstore racks and the old films that were shown at the theatre Saturday nights.

Baldy slowed down suddenly to a walk, stopped by the horses ahead of him. They all hesitated a moment, then followed Tom's lead and turned down a path that led to the canyon river.

"I remember a good place along here," he said, and they splashed and waded to a flat plot of ground with a few bushes leaning over from the slope. Here they swung off and tied the horses, gathering a few small logs and sticks.

"We brought coffee," Wally said, "so as to have a fire." They had brought something else too: a bottle of milky liquor that Tom claimed was tequila.

Gin disagreed on principle. "You're crazy. There never is any tequila in Santa Fé. Every time some bootlegger goes wrong on his gin he sells the batch to cowboys and calls it tequila."

"I brought it myself from Juarez," said Tom. "It ain't gin. If you don't want it, pass it up. I can use it."

Flo said bravely, "Well, I'll try it. I need something new to get cheered up. I don't care what it is. If I get sick they'll have to let me off the trip tomorrow."

"Oh," said Gin, "I didn't say I didn't want it. Hand it over."

They munched sandwiches and cake in silence. Gin tasted the drink and silently admitted that she was wrong. It might not be tequila, but it was something very strange. It had a chilling effect at first, and after each swallow settled down in her stomach like a stubborn little lump of lead before it seemed to melt and spread. The others finished the food before she noticed: there were only three limp jelly sandwiches left.

"You made them," said Flo, unkindly. "Eat 'em. I told you not to. Have more coffee."

"She don't want coffee," Tom interposed. "Give her the bottle."

Flo said in a discouraged tone, "It's having no effect whatever. I thought I could get happy tonight and forget my troubles, but I'm just the same, only worse."

"It always acts like that when you set out for a good one," said Wally. "One night last year I started out for a three-day party and I kept going all night and went to bed in the morning cold sober."

"It's a strange life," Gin suddenly said. She hugged her knees and rocked backward, staring at the sky. "People trying to make themselves crazy with bottles of poison, when everything is all right as it is."

"What's that?" Wally looked worried.

"It's a strange life," she repeated. "Everything is peculiar. Don't you think so? Really, don't you?"

Flo sighed audibly. "Leave her alone; she's off again."

"But it is," Gin persisted. A messianic zeal possessed her: she must convey the message in her soul or die unappeased. The moon, the bushes, the beautiful silent horses, all waited with an understanding patience while she spoke to these scoffers. "It is," she said again. "Here I am sitting by a fire out in the middle of Nature, wearing pants and drinking tequila. I mean here I am, and ten years ago— five years ago—I was living in cities and wearing skirts and now here I am. It's wonderful."

"That's all right," said Tom. "Of course it's wonderful."

"It's so peculiar. Can't you see?" Her eyes filled with tears; her soul filled with a passionate sensibility of life and all its lovely factors; the moon, the fire, the horses.... She stretched out on the ground and put her head on her arm, thinking it over.

Tom rose to his feet, leaned over her, and pulled her gently by the arm. "Come on, Gin. Come on back to town with me and we'll get some more funny thoughts."

She stumbled after him in the dark and let him untie the horse and help her up to the saddle. They cantered most of the way home; as they swung through the narrow streets at the edge of town she peered through the windows, catching quick flashes of lit rooms with quiet women sewing, or standing at stoves, or washing dishes. Suddenly she felt desolate and lonely, envious of these people who had homes and dull quiet duties.

Tom waved her in to the living-room while he led the horses to the corral. "You wait there and think about life."

She sat on his camp cot and reflected. It was a big bare room, with a bearskin and a beaded vest on the wall for decoration. There was a table with a Victrola and several bottles, and on the window-sill there were stacks of the little fifteen-cent magazines with pictures on them of bucking broncos and cheering cowboys in furry chaps. The last of the West was here, in these dude-wranglers with their tall stories and their horses. Now she was sad with a tender melancholy, and somewhat sleepy. What were they all looking for here in the mountains? Why did they come? She shook her head.

"Now," said Tom in the doorway. "What's it all about?" He handed her a glass. "You ought to feel better with this," he said. He sat down next to her on the bed and put his arm around her. "What's eating you?" he asked gently. "Tell me about it and you'll feel better."

Her face buried in his shoulder, she answered, "Nothing. I feel sleepy. I'm all right."

"Sure nothing's the matter?"

Again she shook her head.

"Well," he said, "I think there is. You don't come around as much as you used to. You've been running around with that funny crowd, the queer ones."

"Why, Tom!" With exaggerated indignation, she sat erect and stared at him.

"Sure you are. I saw you at the show the other night with Madden."

"He's not queer," she protested.

"He ain't? Then I don't know anything about queer ones. Take your medicine there."

An hour or so passed in jerks; quick lovely spaces of time with the Victrola playing and short horrible periods that dragged on for years, when she relapsed into stupidity and stared at the beaded vest and tried not to talk about life. She saw Tom once in a while, as it were, looking at her and grinning in a monotonous way: she leaned against his shoulder in an unpleasant spell of dizziness, and it was there that Flo found her when she came stamping in with Wally. She heard Flo's sharp voice.

"Look at that! Did you ever? We'd better get a taxi." And in the car that crept through the dark streets she sat up suddenly and said, "Well, I seem to have done it instead of you."

"You did," said Flo. "Lie down."

"I'm all right." She sat up and tried to put off her remorse until next morning. "Where are the boys?"

"I made them stay at the stable. It's too late for them to come out."

"What time is it?"

"Three o'clock, I think."

The house was squat and ominous in the dark; the moon had long since set. Gin crept to bed by the light of the reading-lamp; she felt somehow that the bright light would outrage the hour. Her head felt very light. It wouldn't next day.

"Flo," she called across the room, after she had settled down. There was something to talk over with Flo. What was it? Too much trouble....

"Oh, for heaven's sake! What is it?"

"I'm perfectly sober," Gin said. There was no challenge and she continued, "But just the same, life's peculiar."

CHAPTER FIVE

Mary and the camp-chair sank down together for two inches. Then the chair squeaked and stopped giving in: it stayed where it was in space, poised above the throng of Santo Domingo Indians and dusty crabby tourists like a throne, disregarded on the pueblo roof.

"Well," she continued, when she was sure the chair had come to rest, "I do know that I'm at my wits' ends. I'm desperate." Casually, she drew a handkerchief out of her raffia bag and folded it over her nose, against the dust.

Bob answered, "You wait until you've talked to Lucy Parker. Don't give up hope at this stage. There's such good material in the boy; you mustn't give up hope." He felt that he hadn't said quite enough, but he was tired. Mary was exactly like a sack when she was in a crowd, he thought a little furtively: limp and useless. Dragging Mary and a camp-chair was very fatiguing. His eyes hurt in the sun but he fought against the impulse to put on the sun-glasses in his vest pocket. Mary looked so odd in hers.

From the plaza beneath there came a confused roaring: a mixture of singing and soft-beating drums where the Indians were dancing to the music of the chorus, heavily overlaid and swamped by a loud conversation going on between people squatting before the house. Bob craned his neck to see over the heads of the Indians who blocked the view. He was trying to find Teddy.

"It's Blake's fault," said Mary, understanding him. "He's always running off like that: this time he's taken Teddy with him. It's very rude of him. I must speak to him again." She readjusted the handkerchief and settled the glasses on her nose. "This dust. I think he's a schizoid personality, don't you? I spoke to Brill about him. If I sell that Patterson property perhaps I might have him analyzed. But he seems so prejudiced against it, and I don't want to force the child. What do you think?"

"Brill? Analysis is a wonderful thing. Yes, that might help." He broke off and waved violently. "There's Lucy now. Lucy! Confound these drums. There, she's coming over." He settled back in relief. He was never at his best with a surrounding audience of less than three or four. He loved people and more people; the more the better. There was no limit to his capacity for company; if he should ever have to live completely alone he would go mad. The frantic boredom that had possessed him with Mary grew more peaceful; slowly and completely died as he watched Lucy pushing a way toward the ladder that leant against their roof. She was followed by her daughter Phyllis and her daughter Phyllis' friend Janie Peabody. Good! Soon there would be activity and noise on the roof around him, and other people would look up to the chattering crowd and say to each other, "That's Bob Stuart."

The three women climbed the ladder carefully, with upheld skirts and cautious feeling of the toes.

"Ah-h-h, Lucy," said Bob lovingly, lending a hand at the last rung. "Phyllis. Miss Peabody. Lucy darling, we were just talking about you. You are to tell Mrs. Lennard everything you know about the California school. She wants to find a school for Blake—you know, Blake."

"My school?" Lucy sat down cross-legged on the roof and lit a cigarette. "Certainly. Tell me if you want it and I'll write you a letter tonight. I should think it would be just the thing for you. Phyllis was such a problem before I sent her there. They always are difficult at a certain age, don't you think?" She turned and flicked an ash at Phyllis, who ignored her by chatting with Janie.

The singing fell to an abrupt end and in the silence shuffling feet were heard. Over an array of backs, fidgeting sweaty backs, they saw green branches jogging, being carried out of the plaza. A fluttering wisp of red shirt moved in the same direction, seen in little jerks as it passed between two fat ladies in khaki hats.

"Oh," cried Mary, "it's over, isn't it? I haven't really seen anything of it."

"No, no," Bob said soothingly. "They start again in a minute. What was all that at your school about psychoanalysis, Lucy? Tell her about it."

"Won't she be bored? I always forget the other people may want to watch the dance. It seems impossible that anyone here could be seeing it for the first time. How many times have we seen it, Bob?"

"Oh, I couldn't say. It's nothing to what it used to be. I remember a dance at Jemez that I stumbled on by sheer accident. It was in the old days when I was collecting. I was taking a trip to San Ysidro to get a blanket—you could still pick up good things in those days. I was driving with poor old Gertrude and we suddenly turned into the village and there it was. Very shocking."

Lucy leaned forward and ground out her cigarette against a stone. The sun was paling as if the air had grown suddenly thick. Behind a high yellow sandy cone back of the town, a black cloud peeped.

"Tell us about it," said Lucy. Down in the plaza the singing swelled triumphantly.

"I couldn't really. They were having something ceremonial and private—I don't know just what. There were baskets of fruit and plates of food; the men made obscene gestures with the bananas. Fertility and all that, I suppose. Gertrude was as white as a sheet; she screamed and drove away as fast as she could, but they didn't pay any attention to us. I was helpless with laughter. You can imagine Gertrude."

"It's a wonderful story," said Lucy. "I should have heard it before. Gertrude never mentioned it to me, but naturally she wouldn't. Well, Mrs. Lennard...."

The singing stopped again.

"Now is it over?"

"No, that's just the end of the first clan's turn. There'll be a lot more before they call it a day.... It's a small school; only a hundred or so, and they have a staff psychoanalyst and all the masters really make a specialty of *understanding* the students. Very modern, of course—you must see the art work. It's coeducational but not in any silly communist way. I mean it's individual. Do you understand what I'm trying to say?"

"I think so. It's very interesting to me, because Blake is such a special case...."

Lucy nodded deeply. "It's a school for special cases; that's the real idea that's behind it all. The woman who founded it is wonderful. I'll give you a letter for her. Oh, look, there's Teddy. Teddy!" She scrambled up and stood on tiptoe, waving. "Of course he'll never be able to hear me with all this noise." The singers were chanting in a high falsetto.

"He's too busy with the courier, mother," said Phyllis. "He can't hear you over all those people. Well, my dear, he was quite angry with me. Have you ever seen him really angry?"

"Never," said Janie.

"I was almost frightened," said Phyllis. "Of course I don't really care what he thinks of me, but it was unpleasant for a few minutes. Tell me what you heard about him in New York."

"Oh, it wasn't anything definite. They talk so in New York, I think. They always say the same thing. I just heard that he gives terribly amusing parties, my dear, with all of that crowd. And no one is quite sure about him because he's seen with people like that all the time: of course no one thinks anything of it any more, and I do think that if a person is amusing I don't think a person's private life ought to have anything to do with it, but what I heard was."

"This atmosphere is simply marvelous for young people," Lucy was telling Mary. "The combination of healthy outdoor life and the peculiar feeling one gets out here of history—the Spaniards, and the Western pioneers, and all that. And the wonderful Indian culture. They imbibe something. Everybody here is so unusually appreciative, haven't you found it so?"

"The only flaw is that we're getting to be so famous," Bob added. "It's ruining the place. I wish the authorities would pass a law prohibiting all these buses and trippers and outsiders. Nothing kills a place as much as the outsiders."

"I feel the same way," said Lucy. "I'm afraid I'm really snobbish about all those visitors. What can they get out of it?"

Jane was saying, "But I'm just going to hold out with what I have until I get back East. You can't tell what people are going to be wearing this fall until you look around. It doesn't matter so much here, but...."

"Do you see Blake anywhere, Bob?" said Mary.

"Don't worry, he'll turn up at the car. He doesn't seem to be with Madden just now."

The crowd was growing sparse. Over the hill beyond the houses cars were leaving in streams, each one silhouetted against the green sky before it crossed the mound and disappeared. As the day faded the land grew wider, more desolate. Under the threatening rain-heavy sky it looked parched and ferocious. Irritated squawks of automobile horns mingled with the thrumming singing voices in the plaza.

Lucy looked down at the people who were hurrying to the cars. "There's Isobel. How very badly she dresses. Have you heard what they're saying about her engagement? Gwen was telling me...."

"Mother says I can go in August if I insist," said Phyllis. "I'm not sure I want to go at all: it's a very dull season, I believe."

"Oh, you *lucky*."

Now there were such a few people left that Blake was in sight, leaning against a ladder at the far corner of the plaza and gazing ahead of him in a bemused way. The dancers were filing out, going in a listless straggling line to the kiva beyond a row of irregularly outlined houses on the other side. The sun was setting behind the clouds and in a few minutes the prayer for rain would be answered. A fresh damp wind was blowing down upon the village.

Green branches and dry rattles carried by the koshare. They walked slowly, now that their work was done, towards the kiva. Beyond the houses they came into sight again, climbing the hard white steps to the roof, pausing against that green sky as they started down the ladder into the round little house. Red shirts and blue shirts followed with the drums, and a low singing went with them.

"But as Gwen says," Lucy finished, "there are times when Isobel is so vague that God knows what really did happen. *She'll* never tell the real story."

Mary stood up and put her glasses back into her bag.

"I'll never forget it," she said. "A most beautiful picture. Absolutely inspiring."

CHAPTER SIX

Again evening had overtaken Santa Fé before anything happened. Every morning Blake woke with a furious desire to get out of the house and down to town, so that he would not miss anything. He never knew what it was that he expected, and day after day developed into the same uneventful solar round. Nevertheless every morning brought with it a tense expectation, a silent waiting.

Tonight he wondered fretfully why the fever was not allayed. It had been a full day, exciting and tiring. The whole town was tired. The drums were still beating in his ears: when he closed his eyes he tried to see the rows of stamping people and the waving branches: but instead he kept thinking of the crowds that filled the village *plaza*; old ladies in felt hats sitting on the roofs, their fat legs dangling over, their fat hands waving to other old ladies on the opposite roofs....

"Missing so much and so much," he murmured, and felt a little revenged.

And the keen young people so greatly to be envied, who knew everything— hatless, collar-less, sparsely bearded young men with folded arms and languid looks; wispy, eager young women; officious, anxious, sweating couriers in jangling silver. And the broad khaki backs of the motor tourists. Around and between them the frantic, shocking, stunning leaps of the ghost-men appearing through the gaps. The drumming in his ears; he was shaken and irritated and cheated: he wanted to cry.

"But our lot crawls between dry ribs to keep its metaphysics warm." Did that have anything to do with it? "Always the appropriate thing." In a gust of fury he kicked a pebble far up the pavement, spinning and skipping.

The waiting was not satisfied. Perhaps he was not, after all, the only one to feel that way. The plaza, dark in the centre but lighted around the sidewalk, was full of people looking for something. It was a small plaza, insufficient for so many prowling people, walking round and round.

In the shadows of the north side he found Madden, lounging on a bench and more or less waiting for him.

"We'll have to go to the cafe," he said, as Blake came up. "Everything else is jammed. I'm not hungry, are you?"

"No. I ate dust all day. Did you smell that jerked meat?"

"Oh, that. You'll get used to that."

They crossed the plot of grass and elbowed through the procession on the walk. The cafe was crowded too. Only half disappointed, they loitered at the door, peering in at the restaurant until they drew a hail from Harvey and Gin, who had a booth.

"Come on over," Harvey said. "Plenty of room." Gin gathered her skirts and edged to the wall invitingly. Blake glowered at her, representative as she was of the whole jostling day.

"I saw you there," she told him, "looking very fierce. I'm sorry. You might have pitied me a little, and you didn't. I know you didn't: I see it in your eye." She smiled teasingly and he felt a little mollified.

Harvey moved his knife and fork to make room for Blue Plate Number Three, and said, "What're you kids doing tonight? We're looking for excitement. Come along? I've got the car."

Teddy suggested the movies. Blake demurred; he tried to explain that he had wasted far too many of his evenings in the movies, but the others didn't understand. He couldn't tell them that the evenings would be rare and strange and historical if they could only manage them properly. Defeated, he followed them to the theatre and watched an ancient railroad cinema.

Oddly enough, it was Harvey who was tainted by his discontent. As they straggled into the street afterwards he said:

"It's always the same thing. Let's get out of the old town. Let's...." he paused.

"Let's go for a ride," Gin said. "There's nothing else."

Certainly there was some surcease in going fast and having nothing to do. Blake sat on the back of the seat, perched on the rolled-up top; the wind was strong with a little bite to it, and he closed his ears and tried to listen without seeing. It was almost perfect. The little lurch his body gave for no apparent reason—that would be a curve in the road. The roaring in his ears that came and went and came again—that must be a canyon. The louder the hum of the car, and a slowing-down of wind that was a hill, and there was a scent the wind that could not be anything but pines growing on the mountain side. Now they turned off on a rough road; he swayed and would have fallen if he had not opened his eyes.

Madden saved him by grabbing his arm; they called to Harvey to go easy.

"We're trying to find our way," Gin shouted over her shoulder. "We're lost."

"I know that already. Say, for Christ's sake...." Madden stopped and seized the side of the car as a bump almost threw him out. Blake slid down to the floor with a jerk, and the engine stopped of its own fatigue.

"Something's wrong," said Harvey. "Something certainly is wrong." He got out and stooped down in front. "High centre. We'll have to dig out. I'm glad I brought the shovel. Where are we anyway?"

No one knew. It was late and getting cold: they huddled down in blankets and decided to wait for the moon before trying to get out.

"This is better than town, anyway," Gin said.

Madden cried indignantly, "What do you mean, anyway? This is *great*. Look at the stars."

It was very quiet. Closing their eyes, they tried to stop shivering. Harvey searched in the side-pockets and found a half bottle of corn, which helped a little. In a sentimental voice, Gin began to sing:

Once in the dear dead days beyond recall When on the world a mist began to fall....

The others joined in, howling away in a canine ecstasy of grief. They were silent afterwards, revelling in a misty regret. Then Madden began,

> Tu eres Lupita divina,
> Como los rayos del sol.

Blake hummed along with him, filling in the gaps in his memory with an ambiguous gibberish. Harvey contributed,

> She'd a dark and roving eye,
> And her hair hung down in ringlets,
> A NICE girl, a DECENT girl (here his voice cracked)
> But one of the rakish kind.

Then they had "Lord Geoffrey Amherst," and in spite of many protests, Gin sang doggedly to the end of "The Sweetheart of Sigma Chi."

To the east there was a pale white glow in the sky, outlining the hills. Blake saw a glimpse of the moon. He cried out his discovery, and the heavy white ball lifted into the sky to the accompaniment of four fresh young voices rising out of the valley, chanting,

"God bless the bastard king of dear old England."

They stirred themselves and began to dig in the sand. After a while they freed the car and it seemed to work all right. Harvey backed it out and retraced his wheel-tracks to the edge of the main road.

"Now where?"

"Anywhere," said Madden, waving grandly. "Out into the world." He hoisted himself up to the back again: Gin followed suit in the front seat, and the three balancing figures jogged and reeled as Harvey drove on toward Taos. It was almost as light as day. They passed one other machine: driving on in the path of the headlight glow they waved and shrieked until a curve cut it off. Blake drummed with his heels on the leather cushion in a burst of exhilaration.

They left the main road and followed the way to Frijoles Canyon. The car went slower, going through rivers with a cautious swoop and turning corners on all four wheels. Long shadows lay across the silver-splashed fields. It seemed impossible that all the light could be coming from the moon, that was now only a little ball swimming in clouds up toward the centre of the sky. Everything but the car was motionless and asleep. Houses with blank dead eyes crouched by the road. No dogs ran out to race with the wheels.

Blake sank back into the corner of the seat. His head dropped: the shadows blurred and the sound of the engine was more stupefying than silence. He reached with stiff fingers for a blanket, curled up in it and fell into a sort of sleep, his elbows braced against shock. In his dream he was still in the car, riding steadily through the river at school or across baked yellow plains, arguing with Dr. Miller. Sometimes he jerked and waked up, glanced worriedly at Gin's head against the cushion ahead of him, and closed his eyes again. The night was fading.

The car stopped and he woke up completely. He sat up, blinking, and stared at Madden, who was kneeling by the ditch and fishing in the water with a hat.

"What is it?"

"We need water," Gin explained. Her bare knees were propped up over the door, and she powdered her nose vigorously. "We couldn't find anything to use for it. I hope that's not your hat?"

"No," he assured her. "It's been kicking around in this car for a long time, I think."

Making no effort to climb out, he watched Harvey pour what water he still had after crossing the road into the radiator. Sullen and efficient, the other two climbed back and sat still. They all looked drowsily at the sky. The moon had faded from silver to white: down on the earth the glow had disappeared and there was no colour anywhere in the rocks. Everything was black or white or grey.

"Like a steel engraving," said Teddy, "but much more so."

They were in a jumble of rock, chalky-white rock that was broken off in great chunks and piled up into mountains. The ditch emptied into a river that crossed the road farther down and crept off into a ravine of thick-growing juniper, black in the thin light.

Gin blurted, "It looks awful. I hate being in canyons."

They agreed not to drive any more. Blake suggested climbing something. They aimlessly picked out a hill and began to crawl up the side, leaving the car somewhat askew in the road. It was easy to get half-way up; there the climb grew steep and difficult. For a little while no one said anything; they worked in deep silence, holding out their hands to help each other whenever they could. When they climbed over the last boulder, they were puffing. They walked to a ledge that faced the east and sat down to wait for the sun, shivering in the wind.

Gin sighed ponderously, lay down with her arm under her head, and went to sleep. Harvey curled up next to her with his arm protectingly over her head. He snored and rubbed his cheek softly against the rock.

"I wonder what time it is," Teddy said to Blake. "I've never felt more awake."

They sat in silence for a time that felt like a century. Their legs hung over the sharp edge of the flat hilltop. Blake kicked softly against the rock and a fine powder sifted down.

"This is swell," he said.

"You bet."

He looked at the cruel edges of the hills and the shadows between them, sinking deeper and deeper in the clefts, and he thought,

"I have only two months." He pushed the shadowy hills out of his mind and thought of the train-ride East, the smell of rooms that had been closed all summer with school books locked up inside, the first classes with roll-calls and reading lists in mimeographed sheets. He felt a little nauseated.

"Mother says I've got to go to some school in September," he said aloud. Before him were the hills again, and Teddy sitting next to him.

"Oh, well," said Teddy, "start worrying in September. This is July."

"That's only two months. I won't go, that's all. I won't."

"Well, don't. Don't ever do anything you don't want to do. Look at me."

"Yes, but you're different. No family."

Teddy was silent a minute and then said, "That's so. It shouldn't make any difference, though, if you really know what you want."

"But I don't. Does anybody? Do you? I just know what I don't want. I'll blow up if I go back to school."

"Sure, I know what I want. I want...." he hesitated, chewing on a pine-needle. "I want time to work in peace, and a chance to see new places. I guess I want money. That would fix things. Then I could really do everything I haven't time for."

"What sort of places would you like to see? India?"

"Yes, and some of Europe, and North Africa. I've always wanted to paint in Algeria."

Feeling guilty, Blake said, "Oh, I've been there. It's not so wonderful."

"You've been there?" said Teddy angrily. "Why, you lucky little fool."

"But of course I've been there. Mother had to go for her health, and of course...."

Madden, oddly excited, shook his fist at the air. "Of course, of course, of course. You people who say 'of course.'"

Blake stared at him, mystified. For a cold moment he thought that perhaps Madden hated him. Then everything seemed to calm down: Teddy laughed and spit the pine-needle down between his dangling feet.

"Come with me when I go away, then," he said, "and see if you can get a kick out of that."

"When?" Blake was eager.

"Oh, I don't know. September's a good time. Call it September. We'll drive somewhere." He shook his head and laughed again. "I'm getting nutty. How can I dig myself out of this hole? Damned cesspool." He closed his eyes against the black and white panorama and went to sleep.

The sky was getting red. In a minute there would be a sunrise: Blake tried to concentrate on it. People never saw the sunrise: people ought to look oftener at sunrises. Even one a month would be better than none at all. Some day he would change the system and live at night: he would finish his day with a sunrise and then go to bed immediately.

Like this. Was it going to be red-orange, or gold? The clouds across the sky, on the other side, were beginning to flush near the sun. Where was the sun? Everything was waiting for it. Somewhere a few miles farther east there must be someone looking at it right now. All day there were sunrises somewhere in the world. A few hours ago there had been one in Algeria, and none of the people in the hotel there would have seen it. There would be a few servants coming to work in white robes growing pink in the red light. But here on this rock in New Mexico one person would watch it. Blake Lennard Watches Sunrise. He pulled his feet up and lay down facing east.

Suddenly the sun was there, but the four huddled bodies on the high rock did not move.

CHAPTER SEVEN

They all woke at once, perhaps because a bird screamed as it flew over them. Teddy sat up so swiftly that he almost toppled off the edge. He stared wildly about him, trying to remember. The other three propped themselves up on their arms, with tousled hair, and faces marked by the rock. It was as if they had been carried to another place while they slept; this was a green country with another sun shining down on it, a second cousin to their sun; small and high and cheerful. He had a confused feeling that he must have been drunk. No one spoke: they were all waiting. Then, as if she could not control herself any longer, Gin giggled.

"Gee, we look funny," she said, and broke the spell. "What time is it?"

No one had a watch. They stood up, groaning and helping each other. One by one, with grim sensible expressions, they disappeared behind a rocky crag. They all used Harvey's little black comb, and slowly worked up enough concerted impulse to climb down the hill. It was not so easy as it had been to climb up.

His shoes scuffed, his toes jammed into the ends of them, Teddy walked blindly over the sand, leading the straggling procession. A luminous exaltation possessed them all, shining from their faces, defying hunger and sleepiness. He tried to put it into words in his mind, in a hysterical stream of phrases.... "Companions of the night ... black wind and the freedom of motion.... Away from the earth, here in fresh-born sunlight, we are new again and shining. The true artist, the true man lies down where he happens to be, like an animal, and sleeps as he wishes...." He stumbled on a sandy hummock and felt a little dizzy.

They climbed stiffly into the car. Gin was obsessed with chatter: she talked of her hunger, her disordered clothes, her lame shoulder, in a gay high voice that had nothing to do with what she was saying. Harvey watched her sombrely and silently. Her hair hung loose around her shoulders: she tried once to twist it up but it fell again: in the wind it streamed out sideways when they started to move, and whipped back, catching Harvey on the cheek. She was beautiful, Teddy thought. He said,

"If you wouldn't turn out to be such a 'Saturday Evening Post' girl, I'd paint you."

"I will anyway," cried Blake. "I'll paint all of us. It will be a frontispiece to 'Treasure Island' and we'll all be disgraced."

"We are disgraced," she cried joyfully. "Paint us, paint us." She leaned over the side as limply as she could, imitating a corpse. "Dead, dead, dead," she murmured. A roadster full of staring tourists passed in the other direction, and swerved as the driver turned for a last look.

"Wheeee, it's late," said Teddy. "When do we eat? How far are we? Where are we?"

Suddenly Gin screamed and then sat still with her fist to her open mouth.

"What's the matter?" they all asked.

"My job! I forgot. How could I?"

"Ooo," said Blake. "And it's late."

"How could I?"

"I think it's charming," Madden answered. "It's darling of you. I love to have people forget important things. It's good for your soul."

She shook her head impatiently, her eyes wet. They were all subdued.

"Take me to a phone," she said suddenly. "As soon as we get to town I'll call the office."

"Don't worry," said Harvey, "Flo probably had a brainstorm and called them already. Is she in town today?"

"I don't know. Well, never mind. Breakfast!"

They came into town with a wild swoop. At the little cafe Gin rushed for the telephone and found that Flo had committed the necessary perjury. She returned radiant to her coffee and fried eggs.

"I've been trying to do a poem all night, I think," Blake was telling Teddy. "I dreamed the beginning of it and added a lot and it was very good. Now I've forgotten most of it." He laughed. "There are just two lines."

Teddy ordered, "Let's have them."

"They're silly. They don't mean anything."

"Well, let's see."

"Just this.

> "Your narrow eyes roaming desireless
> Skim cruelly the arid desert sands.

"There was a picture that went with it of a figure on a mountain top."

"I'll draw it," said Madden.

Harvey snuffled in scorn and looked side-wise at Blake.

"I don't feel at all like going home," said Blake. "We ought to do something else now."

"Let's go to Taos," said Teddy.

Gin cried out in alarm. "You do what you like, but take me home first. I'm down for Lamy this afternoon. Are you trying to ruin me?"

"I'm going to work," Harvey said decidedly. "Let's get going."

They put Gin down first, while she tried feebly to tuck her hair up before she ran into her house. From the depths of the house they heard Flo, shrill and abusive, as they turned the car in the narrow street and headed for the Lennards'. Blake fell silent and thoughtful as they drew near home.

"On second thought," he told Harvey, "it might be wise for me to walk the last few steps. Mother may be excited. I hope she went to sleep." He stepped lightly over the door and advanced bravely to the house: the car turned discreetly and went toward town again.

Harvey was grumpy on the way back. He dumped Teddy at the door of their house and drove away again silently. Already the day seemed tired. Languid and a little depressed, Madden unlocked the door, carried in the warm bottle of milk, and lay down on his bed.

His telephone rang late in the afternoon and woke him. Confused and feeling guilty, he stumbled over to it and answered the call in a cracked, sleepy voice.

"Hello, Hello? Teddy Madden? Dear boy, where have you been? This is Bob."

"Oh, I was asleep. Just a minute— —?" he lit a cigarette. "I say, am I due up there tonight? I've lost track of time."

He was, Bob assured him a little indignantly. Moreover, he was late for tea.

"I'll be right up," he said. He hung up the receiver and before doing anything else, sat quietly in the half-dark, his head in his hands.

"Gosh...." Waves of gloom had overtaken him at last; after being outrun for a week they had caught him. Reasonless, they were; or at any rate he had too many reasons to worry; none at all for this persistent depression. Bills, conscience, perpetual hangover—he ran them over in his mind, but there was no answering twinge as he called them out. It was something else; something that followed every jag of happiness. It was as much a part of this play town as the other, pleasant, excitement: a gnawing whimpering nameless anxiety that was waiting for him whenever he sat alone in the dark. It took gigantic effort to call the cab-stand.

"Harv? Madden calling. Listen, Harv, send a car round right away, will you? Here, of course. No, home. Oh, charge it."

Harvey expostulated in a mechanical, hopeless manner. "I got to tighten up on you, Madden. Listen to reason. Do you know what you owe here?... All right, but if you wait ten minutes, I'll be home and run you up myself. Oh, all right. I'll send Ben: he's turning into the yard now."

"Thanks. Look, I'll pay right now."

"You and who else?" asked his room-mate wearily.

Turning into the Stuart driveway, however, he solved the problem. Bob was standing on the porch superintending the parking of another car, and strolled down to meet the taxi.

"Got any change, Bob?" asked Madden: and the two bits were forthcoming. He walked into the house with a virtuous feeling, into a small crowd of people.

Mrs. Saville-Sanders was perched on a window-seat, holding forth to Mrs. Lyons and a strange woman in a hat. Mrs. Lennard was talking to Phil Ray and stopped to smile at Teddy as he entered. Nothing wrong in that quarter, then: Blake was all right. There were other people just coming in; not very good friends of Bob, to judge by his attitude. Teddy poured himself a drink and sat down by Mrs. Lyons, who patted his arm in greeting.

She was a nice old thing, he told himself again. She was one of the few stands he took against public opinion. Most of the people in Santa Fé, that is, the people he ran with, made fun of her. She was not quite bright, they argued. It was always just a few minutes before they said anything really serious that Teddy would protest,

"Well, I like old Ruth."

He really did. She was kindly, credulous and restful. She was generous. She was maternal. If she was a little smug, the only difference between her attitude and Mrs. Saville-Sanders', he said to himself, was that she had less money to be smug about. The other thing was that she was a native daughter and had a tangible husband. He was a popular artist who took himself quite seriously and made a cottage-and-garden living by executing big colourful murals of Indians wearing the wrong kind of moccasins and shooting arrows at conventionalized mesas with all of the shadows on the same side.

Teddy would say, "Of course, Tommy's *work*—but I like old Ruth."

Gwendolyn Saville-Sanders was busy getting people to do something about Santa Fé. Gwendolyn, unlike old Ruth, had been coming out here for only three years. Before the war did so many horrible things to it, she had spent her leisure and a lot more in Fiesole: before she was told about Fiesole it had been Switzerland. But Gwendolyn had begun to take up America in a serious manner. She was a little behind other people in doing it: many others had brought back treasures of Indian handicraft to their Eastern homes before she had seen the writing on the wall and hastened out to Art's new headquarters. Now that she had found it, though, she was making the most of it. Gwendolyn was slow on the uptake, but thorough. Her three years of discovery had been swift and ferocious: already her collection of Navajo silver was the largest in America (not counting the museums) and her Chimayo blankets were famous. As for the tin candle-sconces, it was no less than wonderful, the number she had salvaged in the short time she had had.

No necessity here for Teddy to say, "Well, I don't care, I like old Gwen." One liked Gwen as a matter of course. As soon as she left a room, becomingly cheerful in farewell, one murmured, "Isn't she marvelous?" or, "Isn't she perfectly grand?" The thing that counted in this matter was that Gwendolyn should say after you yourself had left the room,

"I like that Teddy. He's a nice boy."

As yet she had not said it, at least Bob had not reported it. So Teddy sat down next to Ruth Lyons and listened.

She was steamed up about Fiesta.

"I think that we need something for the last night, to raise the curtain on the Ball," she was saying. "I think that a bazaar might be the thing, or a play. Why don't you write a play, Teddy?" Her voice, terrifyingly loud, rang out through the room and everyone turned to listen. That was what she wanted. "Write a play," she insisted. "You bright young people! You can do it. Write a play and I'll put it on in my garden."

"Your wish is my command, old thing," he said. Bob walked over and swung an arm around his shoulders, saying,

"That's the right spirit, Teddy. We'll all help."

Gwen smiled and changed her mind. "Or a vaudeville. A vaudeville would be easier and we'd please more people. Ruth, you must tell Tommy to do the sets— we'll get *all* the artists to do the sets. And the Native Element will be able to help. They're so histrionic. The Indians and the Spaniards and all that. Is that settled? Good: I must go. Bob darling, pick out a committee. I must go. Where did I put my bag? It's all settled then; a play. No, a vaudeville. I *must* go. Teddy, come to lunch tomorrow. Good-night, Ruth. Goodbye, everybody, I must simply fly."

They all flew except Teddy and Philip and the stranger with the hat. They were going to dine, Bob said, and then play bridge. The stranger was a puzzled frightened woman from Austria who had come over to paint Indians. She was going on to Japan to paint cherry-blossoms. The Indians were an interlude between cherry-blossoms in Japan and chestnut blossoms in Paris. Teddy remembered seeing some of her work in the Modern Wing of the Museum; he had thought then for a few stormy moments that they had no business being there, and now, looking at her, he was sure of it. She was open-mouthed and passive under an onslaught of information. Bob loved to give information about his country.

In the dining-room they chatted thus: Bob shining with happiness. His dour Mexican maid served the soup.

"You have mountains too, of course," he said, and Miss Kolbenhayer nodded. "But I always think that it is not the mere rocks and stones and trees that make the mountains. Here we have something else to contend with: the smouldering forces of the American Indian."

Miss Kolbenhayer's soup-spoon stopped at the edge of her plate. "But here they are quite tame, is it not so?"

"Unfortunately they are, for the most part," he admitted. "It is the mixed breed that is prone to strange outbursts. Things go on here ... religious frenzies ... crimes of innocence.... I suppose no one had told you of the Red River crime?"

No one had.

"Now, there's an instance." Bob gave up the soup proposition for the evening. "A girl from the East with her newly married husband and a guide went on a hunting north of here. They met a sheep-herder, a Mexican. A mere boy; sixteen, I think. He came up to their camp-fire one night. It is the law of the mountains: they gave him food. The next morning he went on with them and they gave him a gun to carry. Now, he had noticed the girl, and he wanted her." Bob bit ferociously into the cracker and repeated, "Wanted her. So he shot the husband." He stared at Miss Kolbenhayer.

Flo twisted around and looked, "Hmmm. Shot the husband and the guide. They died immediately."

"Oh!"

"Immediately. The girl ran seven miles to Red River, where she sobbed out her story and fainted." Bob's round little face beamed with pride. "The strangest thing is what the sheep-herder said at the trial. When they asked him if he had anything to offer in defence he said that the devil had entered his soul. In a way he was right, poor chap."

Miss Kolbenhayer shuddered. "It's like your Chicago."

"Oh, Chicago," said Bob in scorn. "That is a commercial city. The crimes are commercial and stupid. Here we are faced with a mysterious people."

He hesitated as Revelita changed the plates, and Teddy fell into a revery that had to do with the mysterious people. In the old foolish days when he had first come and had been overwhelmed by the place, he had tried to plunge headlong into the native life of the town. There had been dances in the little halls at the edge of the city: colourful but stiff affairs with little skinny girls wearing pink ribbons in their hair, dancing with swarthy little boys. He had eaten by preference in the Mexican restaurants—not that there were many; the native townspeople liked to eat at home—where he had tried to burn out his guts, as he expressed it, with chile in various forms. Here and there he met and danced with Revelita.

Then came the new phase, when he began to go uptown to the big houses. He had almost forgotten the queer triumphant feeling he had when Revelita first appeared at his elbow at Bob's, wearing a white apron and offering him a cocktail from a tray, eyes downcast, and lips composed. Then the climax, a few nights later, when he was alone in Bob's house, drawing upon his new pleasant intimacy by reading in the library while Bob was out at Sanford's. The hurried step outside, the Spanish recriminations, and Revelita's startled face when she found him in a supposedly empty house; her face still twisted in anger and fear of her father, who had beaten her after a quarrel, and driven her up to Bob's strap in hand. Of course, something had to be done to quiet her. Together, amused by the piquancy of it, they raided the liquor-chest. Revelita was reckless, drunk, excited out of her usual reserve. Followed the usual row of asterisks, he told himself. And then the next day she appeared once more at his elbow in the white apron, eyes downcast, lips composed. He still remembered the thrill of power that little incident had given him. It was a wonderful town.

"A mysterious people." Bob repeated as Revelita's stocky figure passed out through the door. "Who knows what they are thinking?"

They had coffee in the living-room before beginning to play. Teddy looked around at the calm well-fed faces, the heavy blankets that curtained the windows, the polished floor and all the big permanent things that Stuart lived with, among which he had his leisurely thoughts of people and poetry and music.

Quietly, he stretched out his legs and settled back to sip the coffee. For the first time that day, he was really happy. Safe.

CHAPTER EIGHT

"I think I'm going crazy," Flo remarked in a pleased tone. "I've thought so several times lately and there's no possible doubt."

"Huh?" said Gin. She turned a page of the new "Photoplay" and cried suddenly, "*Look* at this! I'll never speak to him again!"

"Who?"

"Clive Brook. Oh, dear, he's wearing the most godawful waistcoat. Look."

"Tasty, I think. Pour me some tea, that's a good girl."

"Why do you think you are going crazy? I want some more chocolate cake. Where is that girl?"

"She'll be here in a minute…. Because I keep forgetting things: today I forgot to say anything to my people all the way back to Puye. I didn't go to sleep exactly: I just forgot. I didn't tell them to turn their tickets in to the office and Margaret was furious because she had to call up all the rooms, and some of them weren't in their rooms and she had to write dozens of notes."

"Lazy old thing. It'll do her good. I get those vague streaks sometimes myself."

"Oh, *you*, it's always a hangover with you…. Who's that across the street?"

Gin stood up to see over the drapes. "It's that new fiancee of Bill Trewarth's. She comes from Carolina or somewhere."

"She looks cute. I wonder what it would be like to go visiting for a whole summer just because you are somebody's fiancee."

"I think it would feel very musty. You would be going to teas with his mother most of the time and on Sunday if you were very good he'd take you out to watch the polo."

Flo powdered her nose and considered. "I think it would be nice," she said. "No responsibility."

"My God! You don't mean it…. Hey, you, I want another piece of cake. You can't mean it. Did you ever hear them talking?"

"Sure I have. Well, what *else* is there to do?"

"This, or something like this in some other place. Why not?"

"But then what about men?"

"Haven't you enough men, for heavens' sake? *Those* dumb brutes."

"No, I haven't, and neither have you. You know perfectly well I haven't: there aren't enough to go round in this town."

Gin admitted that there were not enough men. "But," she added, "it's a law of nature in resort places. You can always go somewhere else if that's all that's worrying you. The question is, what do you really want?"

"Oh," said Flo, passionately, "I want a lot. I want to be rich and stupid like that little beast over there, and I want to be intelligent and interesting and comfortable like lots of the people around, and I'd very much like to be wicked and always wear black. The question is, what am I going to get? I'm tired of this sort of thing. At this rate I'll start looking for Life, and then I'll be a dirty little pushover like Rita."

"Why, Flo. Such language. You couldn't be anyway, you're not the type; you're older than Rita. Anyway, she's not a dirty little pushover. She just doesn't worry about things. She has a good time."

"Really. I suppose you'd say I'd be better off if I *were* the type?"

"Good heavens," said Gin impatiently. "I'm not advising you. I feel like a mess myself, lots of times. I hate Rita as much as you do, and you know it. Even if I could act that way I wouldn't: I'm not sure I even want to. But what can you do about it? The trouble with you is——"

"Your cigarette went out," said Flo. "Yes, darling, what *is* the trouble with me?"

"You're feeling your oats," said Gin. "It makes you expect too much of the world, feeling your oats. You can't help thinking there must be something to do about it. There isn't; because whatever you do about it, it's not settled."

"Where did you find all this out, Grandma?"

"Well," said Gin. "I tried a lot of things and what I didn't try, somebody else did. This town is full of people who try to do something about it. Only the dumb ones have a good time at all. People who believe they are being noble, like Rex and Ada living together. Just the idea that they are being bad keeps them going: they won't have to do another thing all their lives. They're living up to a principle."

"But nobody cares."

"Well, how do they know that? They're happy and they give us something to tell the dudes about. I've got to go home. Where do you go tomorrow? Have you looked at the chart?"

"They haven't decided yet about Mesa Verde. If I do go, I won't have enough clean shirts. How many could you lend me in an emergency?"

"Only one. Don't let me catch you taking more. I may be sent somewhere myself."

They paid the bill, scrupulously dividing it, and walked home in silence. As they turned in the gate Flo said,

"Well, I'm going to do something. I'm going to get engaged."

"Yes? Who to?"

"I don't know. I probably haven't met him yet, but I'm going to get engaged pretty soon. What's more, I'm going to get married." She threw her hat into the closet. "To the next man I meet, if I can. There must be something in it because so many people do it."

"Well," Gin said, "it's a big risk, I think. But I guess it's your own business." She thought about it for a long time while she rubbed cold cream on her face, in the bathroom. "Are you going to get a man with a mother, so you can visit her next summer?" she called through the open door.

"If I can," was the candid retort. Gin frowned into the mirror and began to apply a waver to her hair. After a tense moment of arranging the lock over the left temple she shouted,

"Try to get a dude."

"I've never yet had an unmarried man on the Detour," said Flo solemnly.

"Well, then, a driver. Keep it in the family. There's always at least one who has just had a divorce." There was no answer to this. She tried again: "Write to the papers."

"Oh, shut up. I'm serious, I tell you."

"Well, you should be. It's no laughing matter. Can I borrow a brassiere?"

"No."

"Oh, go on and get married. I think it's a swell idea. Name the first one after me and I'll send it a rattle. Can I borrow a brassiere?"

"There's one in the bottom drawer."

"You'd better start buying a lot of brassieres," Gin called, after inspecting the supply in the lower drawer. "Most of yours aren't the right kind."

"What do you mean?"

"You'd better buy a lot because girls who get engaged always wear very tight ones. Haven't you noticed? They never flop. They don't have to."

"You're vulgar," said Flo.

"No, really. It ought to be one of the first things into the hope chest."

There was a disgusted silence. She finished dressing, though one of her stockings had a run and it took a long time to find another pair. She felt jumpy, and it wasn't nearly seven, when Harvey was to call for her. Swishing into the living room, she picked up a "Photoplay" and tried to settle down, but she kept thinking of Flo. Flo was smoking and reading and looking very determined.

"You're all dressed up too," Gin said at last, trying to ignore the chill in the room. She thought that she sounded much too bright and conciliatory, but something had to be done. "What's on?"

"Beetie wants me to come up and play bridge," Flo said. "I don't know who else is going to be there—one is Russell somebody, the new real estate man—but I didn't want to take chances on looking tacky."

There now: things were more comfortable. Gin turned back to her magazine in peace. Harvey was five minutes early, and in a jovial mood. The door was open, but he rang the shrill bell and called,

"Hello, hello!"

When he saw Flo he calmed down a little; he never seemed to like her. Gin was always nervous when they had to talk to each other; they both acted too polite. Perhaps she shouldn't have told Flo so much about him. Flo was a prude. Now she put on her coat and hurried him out as fast as she could.

"What's new?" asked Harvey. He turned off on the Vegas road and speeded up.

"Oh, nothing, I think they'll send me to Albuquerque tomorrow: that means I'll stay down overnight to meet the morning trains. I hope it won't be too hot to sleep."

"Overnight? I hope you don't go. The Summerses are throwing a party tomorrow night and told me to bring you."

"Oh, I don't mind missing it. I get bored at those parties. The same old jokes and the same old people getting tight. Now where are we going?"

"Pecos," he said. "I feel like having a steak. Do you mind?"

"Nope. Go ahead."

Absorbed in speeding, he grew taciturn, but Gin didn't care. She sat back and stared at the road, trying to stop watching for bumps. That was the trouble with learning to drive; it ruined you as a passenger. With an effort she looked away from the spot of light that the car was pursuing, and stared at the side of the road. They were running by the railroad track. In the daytime, riding in the big passenger buses, the road was so familiar that she hated it, but now it was too dark to be anything but a dangerous path that might at any minute lurch towards the train tracks and carry them straight into the way of destruction. Once a bus had driven out too far on a soft shoulder, and had toppled over. The courier's leg was hurt and a passenger broke a rib. If a train had come by.... She could hear a train chugging up the mountain. She half turned and saw a far-off glow. The road curved and looped and swept towards the track, and then away from it. The train was coming close ... closer ... closer ... perhaps now, just before it reached them, they would drive into its path. Harvey didn't care. He went on just as fast as before.

A straining moment, then they were out of danger and the monster was neck and neck with them, puffing, shrieking, grinding, giving her a horrible close glimpse of its insides and an idea of what might have happened. Harvey stepped on the gas and for a moment they stayed together, then the train pulled ahead slowly, seemed to gather speed, marched by dragging a long tail spotted with square windows, and swung around a curve ahead to vanish forever. Only the smoke hung in the air and mixed with the smell of gasoline and burning cedar.

"What's the matter with you?" said Harvey. "You're pinching my arm."

"Just playing," she said, and moved over to her own side of the car again.

They reached Pecos hungry and a little chilled. There was a roadhouse nearby where people would stop for gas and, if they knew anything about the country, for food. They ate a leisurely dinner, chatting with the waitress and playing the two records that were not warped or cracked—"The Big Rock Candy Mountain" and "Two Black Crows, Part III." Driving home afterwards, Harvey went slower, surfeited with beefsteak. He slowed up outside of Beetie's house, at Gin's suggestion, and they peered through the windows to see if there was any possibility of joining in. Beetie and Flo had their noses in their cards, and their partners were two young men that Gin had never seen before.

"Do you want to crash it?" asked Harvey. "It looks dead. I can't get very thrilled about it myself. Let's go home and see what Madden's up to."

"Oh, he'll be up at Stuart's."

"Maybe not. We'll look."

There was no one in the little house, but a log was still burning in the fireplace and Teddy had left dirty dishes on the table. A new unframed picture was hanging on the wall. Gin examined it. There were two mountains, one leaning over the other, and three adobe houses with red chile hanging from the roofs, making bands of red.

"Oh, did you hear about that?" said Harvey. "Mrs. Lennard is buying it for a hundred dollars. At least I think that's the one. There are so many like it, around here."

"How marvelous for Teddy!"

"Yeah, Madden owes about three times that much. I don't see why he doesn't get a little sense and go to work. This new vaudeville business will keep him going for another month if they pay him anything."

"Well, they ought to," said Gin. "He'll probably work his head off fixing it up." She kicked a coal farther into the fire and stood on the hearth, musing. How did people keep going when they owed money that way? It worried her to owe money. Once when she forgot the bill for kindling they wouldn't send the next order and she had to find another coal company until it was fixed up. It had been awfully embarrassing. Madden just went on charging things and charging things. If she could go on like that without worrying, she might enjoy things a lot more. It was partly Flo's fault that she was that way: Flo was scared of getting into debt: she actually kept money in the bank.

"I couldn't ever be an artist," she said. "I'd be too worried all the time."

"Oh, he gets along." Harvey sat down on the camp cot nearest the fire; the one with the Yeibichai design on the blanket. "Sit down and be sociable."

She sat next to him and he put one arm around her while he held on to his pipe with the other hand, puffing steadily.

"Slow place, isn't it?" he said.

"I guess so. I don't mind much. I like the country."

"Yeah, I do too. But you ought to see Colorado; it's got this skinned a mile."

"You come from Colorado, don't you?"

He nodded. "Dad's there now. I've got an old horse that I broke in myself; he's still up there." He took his arm away to light his pipe again, then put it back and squeezed her under the arm with his hand. As if he didn't notice.... "When I go back he always knows me. I taught him to dance: I used to have ideas about taking him on the stage. He sure was a pretty pony. Getting old now."

She was drowsy from looking so long at the fire. There was nothing to say anyway. Harvey had told all the stories that you tell people you've just met; they knew each other too well to have any conversation. Unless they talked about philosophy, and he didn't like to do that. He always said she thought too much, probably because he didn't want to bother about thinking. She yawned; he went on smoking. The room was getting warm and pleasantly stuffy.

When his pipe was finished he knocked it out on the edge of the fireplace and put both arms around her. They kissed, and he hugged her tighter and tighter and then, just as their lips separated, he tried to make her lie down.

"No," she said uneasily, and pushed him away. He stopped and she felt ridiculously stiff and upright. She leaned forward with her elbows on her knees.

"What's the matter with you tonight?" he asked, not unreasonably. She didn't say anything because she didn't want to explain this sensation of wariness. Two or three times before she had spent the whole evening lying with him on the couch, fondling more or less innocuously. She felt now—she didn't say it even to herself, but she felt that it was time for something more to happen. She had been brought up in the belief that it was up to her, as the control element in the game, to keep a watchful eye on developments and to manage when it came to necking. They started it and did their best to let it run its own course. They deliberately forgot what they were doing. And then if anything definite happened, everybody knew they always felt sorry and wished it hadn't happened. So it was up to her to remember.

"Well?" said Harvey.

"I don't feel like it," she said.

"Sure you do. Come on." He pulled her down and she lay next to him rigid and watchful. He kissed her again.

"God, you're cold tonight."

"Well, I told you."

"Want a drink?"

"No."

He tried to make her open her lips. She was stubborn and in the struggle they both laughed and she relented a little. In a stupid, urgent way he made love to her while she waited passively and grew more and more irritated. He was so easy to see through. Trying to make her forget, trying to deny all her intelligence, trying to sneak. It was worse than when he just sort of went to sleep and breathed hard and forgot anything except that she was a body next to him to clutch and hold tight. She suddenly jerked away from him and sat up, patting her hair. Her cheeks burned because his whiskers had scratched them.

"Aw, Gin!" He lay watching her for a minute, and then he too sat up, with his necktie all crooked. She was angry and a little disgusted.

"Damn you," he said.

"Well, I told you. I told you."

He didn't answer. Feeling miserable and guilty, she walked over to her coat and rummaged in the pocket for a comb. She primped and patted herself with defiant jerky movements, and wished that he would speak. He didn't. It swept over her that she didn't really know him at all. She didn't really know anyone. She was alone in Santa Fé, in the universe. Everybody else was hostile and stupid and silent.

"I'm going home," she said at last.

"I think I'd better not see you any more," he answered, as if that were an answer.

"All right, if you think so," she said coldly. "It's up to you." It would be dull, not having him around to take her to parties.

"No, it's up to you."

"Well, then, why shouldn't we see each other? I'm not mad."

"That isn't it," he said. "We've got to do something about it."

"About what?"

"Don't be dumb." He seemed to feel more cheerful now. He was filling his pipe again, but was still sulky.

"Well, we aren't ever going to do anything about it, then," she said decidedly.

He shrugged his shoulders. "Good-bye, then, I guess you can get home all right."

"Good-bye," she said. In a rush of remorse, she paused at the door. "Honestly, is that the way you feel about it?" she asked. "Didn't you ever just like me?"

"Well, Jesus Christ, Gin," he cried. "You're a girl. How did you expect me to feel?"

"I don't know," she said miserably. "I thought maybe it wasn't bad, just playing around. Can't I ever have any friends unless I sleep with them? You pretended to like me."

"I can't see it that way. You see," he said carefully, "I've got plenty of *friends*. Fellows. I wanted a girl. It's too much trouble, having a girl for a friend. That isn't what a girl is for. I mean, why take the trouble?"

"Oh," she said. She hesitated, looking out the open door at the road. "Well, then...." she paused. He said nothing. "Well, then. I didn't know that was how you felt."

"Everybody feels that way, I should think," he said.

"Oh! I'm sorry. Well, then ... goodbye."

"Good-bye," he said. He didn't even stand up. "Take care of yourself," he added suddenly, and then he looked away for as long as the door was still open.

She walked as fast as she could, trying to start thinking about something. She couldn't think. She was feeling numb and stupid. If she started to think there would be too much in her mind. But something must be done. Something would have to happen in a minute. She almost ran down the street, away from the house. Her own fault for going out with him at all. She should never have gone out with him or with anybody unless she was going to sleep with them ultimately. Letting them take her to dinner, fooling them and riding around in their cars just on the strength of a false promise. That was the way they all felt.... Wasn't there anyone who just liked her? Was there anyone who felt the way she did, just going along without making plans about getting things from other people? Just talking and letting things happen? She stumbled on a rock in the road, and kicked it furiously aside. Crossing a bridge at the aqueduct, she stopped for breath, and felt tears on her cheeks. She must have been making a noise all the way along the road. How horrible. Everything. How shameful. As soon as he saw it was no use he didn't even take her home. Well, if that was nature.... But what a lonely world. *Everybody*.... Perhaps even old Mr. Dunstan. After this it wouldn't be right for Mr. Dunstan to buy her Coca Colas when she met him in the plaza.

A car ran across the bridge and almost grazed her; its driver did not see her in the dark. It was very late. She blew her nose at last and it was as if she blew all her thoughts, too, into the handkerchief. She tiptoed into the house, but Flo was awake, propped up in her bed, with a book and a Hershey bar.

"What's the matter?" said Flo. "You've been crying. Or shouldn't I notice?"

"I'm sore at everybody," said Gin. She walked over to her bed and began to take off her shoes. "No," she said suddenly. "I'm damned if I'll just go to bed. Let's go out for a walk."

"What? You're crazy. Tell me what's happened."

"Oh, Harvey makes me so sick. Everybody makes me sick. He said I was just good to sleep with."

"Um. How does he know?"

"Don't be an idiot. He says I'm not good for anything else."

"Oh, never mind. I always did think he was pretty low."

"But he's right, Flo. He's right." Her voice rose to a tragic squeak. "That's what's so terrible. That's the way things are."

Flo put down her book and looked benign. "How many times must I tell you about these people? You overrate everybody. You haven't any discrimination at all. The idea of letting a taxi-driver with the brains of a peanut get you so excited. You're shaking all over. Why, he's just one of those people. Good Lord, Gin.... I've half a mind to go with you and walk it off."

"Well, come on. Put something on over your pajamas. Nobody's going to see you."

Flo, surprisingly, acted on the suggestion. She pulled on a skirt and a pair of sandals, then shrouded herself in a coat. "All right, kid," she said. "Let's go. You look like Lady Macbeth."

This was better. Flo was decent all right. It was thrilling, walking through the empty streets. If anyone should stop them and see those pajama-legs dragging! She giggled. They turned to the edge of town and walked up to the top of a hill, making a dust that was invisible in the dark but tickled their noses. At the top they stopped to puff and to look back at the city. There were still some lights; the square of lights that marked the penitentiary and the dimmed lamp posts on the plaza. As they watched, even these went out and left only the moon and a few sparks from the windows of the houses. Now that Gin's heart had stopped beating so fast, she could smell the night smells.

"Oh, well," she said, "to hell with Harvey."

"Sure," said Flo.

CHAPTER NINE

Walking goes in two-four time, but riding either on horse or in an automobile makes a rhythm like a waltz. For half an hour Blake had been thinking up waltzes and trying to hum them against the waltz that his mind seemed to prefer. Whenever he relaxed for the shortest space of time he would hear again, like a stubborn gramophone far back between his ears,

It's three o'clock in the morning:
We've danced—th' whole night through....

and the tick of the left rear wheel of the car kept it up.

Talking was useless; it was impossible to talk except at certain times of the day. Just after breakfast, when they started out, everyone was talkative for an hour. Then they fell silent until lunch, wherever that might happen to be. Afterwards the four people were dead quiet until they had stopped for the night, except for little interludes when Gwendolyn Saville-Sanders would say,

"Do look at that hill over there. Marvelous."

Or Mary would call, "Blake, dear. Not quite so fast. You can never tell who's coming around the curve." When Teddy was driving she didn't worry. Only relatives are unsafe as chauffeurs.

The left rear wheel ticked and Blake hummed waltzes and all the time the road was leading them farther and farther from any place that he had ever been. He felt great. He paid no attention to gas and oil and air. Teddy took care of all that, with the jealous love of a childless woman who has borrowed a nephew for the week. For Blake, stopping for gas and oil was a rude interruption. He would be far off somewhere and suddenly the car would stop in front of a dusty little red pump sitting in the middle of the landscape, with a man in overalls shambling out of the dusty little house behind it. Then Gwendolyn would order soda pop all around, and mop her face. Or she would ask for the ladies' room in a husky whisper that made Blake ashamed to go to his side of the little house.

In between the road was a broad highway, not good enough to let you forget the driving. One pass through the mountains kept Mrs. Saville-Sanders twittering for a long time, but most of the way was on flat ground with the mountains on either side and a long way ahead. He liked it better that way. They were not like California mountains. They were flat on top, and not so blue. Some of them were red and the other colour was a dull yellow. Once they met a man on horseback who was dressed like a Mexican but looked darker. A Navajo? Probably. Later they saw a flock of sheep, and Gwendolyn's ecstatic cry called their eyes to the distant figure, herding them. Yes, it was a Navajo woman in full skirt. They passed a collection of brown buildings with huts like bee-hives scattered around them, and flaunting signs announcing that this was a Navajo trading-post where one could buy real genuine Navajo blankets and silver rings made right there on the premises. At this place they all sniffed, and Teddy stepped on the gas.

Towards Shiprock, the road turned bad. An hour of bumping and floating in the air above the back seat brought from Mary a flat decision that they would stay at Shiprock, if they ever got there.

"The Navajo may be very picturesque," she said, "but we'll do something dreadful to the car if we treat it like this. Don't the springs give way sometimes? Oh, Teddy, didn't you see that bump? No, Blake, we'll stay at Shiprock. Goodness knows what we'd find beyond it, anyway." She broke off and clutched at her hat, bouncing miserably.

Blake was in despair. He knew that it was no use to remonstrate: especially as even Teddy seemed to agree. Teddy was never any good in a free-for-all; he always took Mary's side. Blake didn't think of criticizing him for it. Teddy was simply sometimes a baffling adult and sometimes a companion. It was all in the way you caught him. He himself, still dependent on adult decisions, accepted his bad luck without question.

They found Shiprock at evening, and left Mary and Gwendolyn in their rooms while they strolled around the town, staring. It was thus they came across the truck-driver who was willing to take passengers into the country with him. He was chatting with the owner of one of the trading-posts, and he asked them about the roads.

"They were fine until we got here," Blake said, aggrieved. "Now the trip's over. He" —with a nod at Teddy—"backed out."

The truck-driver pushed his hat back. "He's got sense," he said. "You don't want to go driving these roads if you don't know 'em. Where were you aiming to go?"

"Oh, around," said Teddy. "To see the country. We've got a couple of women who want to stop, that's the trouble. They think it's just as good right here."

"They think they've had their trip," said Blake. "They want to rest here a few days."

"Well, say," said the driver. "Come on with me. I'll drop you off at Clearwater, if you like, and you can catch the mail truck back on Wednesday. There's plenty room in the car."

"Where's Clearwater?" Blake asked eagerly.

"Oh, it's fifty mile out. You'll get a sight of the country going up there. I start at ten tomorrow morning soon as I get loaded. Take it or leave it."

They took it immediately, and hurried home to argue with the ladies.

It was raining when they started, and McLean swore in a cheerful mechanical manner. "We won't make any time worth bragging about," he said.

For a long time they drove down a mere path across flat country, but when the road started to climb they entered a pine wood. It was lovely in the rain; clear spaces were bright green and under the trees the ground was brown and clean-looking. McLean said it was bear country. They saw no bear, but sometimes a rabbit ran ahead of them, scurrying from side to side of the road and just missing death when he achieved the idea of diving into the underbrush. Now and then they slowed up to let the tail end of a flock of sheep and goats go by, scrambling and crowding and making silly noises and poisoning the air with their stench. Sometimes a Navajo cantered past on horseback, raising his hand in salute and for a moment skipping the steady beat of his whip on the horses' flanks.

The truck panted louder, hesitated, ploughed ahead on a momentary level and groaned in a humming falsetto above the grind of the engine.

"She's a bitch of a hill," said McLean.

There was a view. Hills rolled out from the cliff below them, and dropped away to a streaked valley that showed far off where it was not raining; where a dry butte sat placidly in the golden light. The roof of the truck dripped dismally. Down again with dragging brakes and slow turns; Blake caught his breath at every blind corner, forgetting that they would not meet any other cars. The other side of the mountains sent them spinning off into a red country lined with severe rocky hills, and for a long time they rode through the valley, following roads with what seemed to him an utter disregard of direction. All the roads looked alike: two parallel strips of bare soil through the rabbit-brush. But Mac said that any wrong turning would take them, after painful windings, to the door of an Indian house (hogan, he called it) and then they would have to find the way back and start over. Crossing a narrow bit of clay land that bordered a stream, the heavy truck slipped and slid down and churned away helplessly. Mac swore and climbed out, pulling a shovel after him. He beckoned to the boys and they all worked furiously, carrying stones to pack down under the wheels. After an hour they backed out and started on.

Panting, his hands and knees covered with drying mud, his stomach growling in hunger, Blake nevertheless felt glad of the accident. He had met with disaster and overcome the elements. It was his country, as it was the country of the dark men and the garrulous cheerful truck-driver. This was the place he had come out West for. In these quiet wild valleys he forgot even the search. Now, riding at dusk in a muddy truck, he forgot the boy in Santa Fé ceaselessly looking for something.

Clearwater was three buildings square and neat in the middle of a clearing; built partly of trimmed stone and partly of logs. The storehouse looked like a barracks; the trader's house was the same except that there were lights in the windows and a big dog tied to the door and a red-haired boy standing by him. He ran towards the truck, crying,

"Mac, Mac! Dad killed a rattlesnake in the henhouse. It almost bit Ma. Who's with you?" When he saw strangers he grew quiet and stood motionless. Mac threw him a bag.

"Catch, Buddy. Where's your Dad?"

They pushed open the screen door, passed the growling dog, and entered a bare ugly room with sacks piled in the corners. Beyond this was a living-room with stiff blue plush furniture, and a woman hurrying through the other door to meet them.

"Evening, Mac." She rubbed her hands down her flat hips and looked shyly at the boys.

"Evening, Mrs. Bush. Can you put the boys up for a couple of days? I figured Warren would stop by Wednesday, so I brought 'em along."

"That's right. Come in and eat; Jim'll be here in a minute. He's looking up the store. Come on in; I was just dishing supper."

They followed her to the next room, where an oil lamp burned on a spread table. The rest of the room was shadowy, but Blake saw a radio against one wall. Mac sat down and they joined him. The boy lurked in the corner, studying them. When his father came in he darted behind him. Bush was a tall blond man with a brown face, inflexible and expressionless. He shook hands mutely with each of the boys when they were introduced by Mac, and they each stood up. Mrs. Bush came in with a tray of beef stew and canned peaches and mashed potatoes and they all started to cat, silently.

With the food and warmth, Blake began to overcome his first feeling of strangeness. The little-boy fear of sleeping away from home was ebbing and he thought that perhaps he was growing up at last. He even managed to ask for a second helping of stew, but to join in the slowly increasing conversation was an effort too much for him. Bush asked Mac about the trip and was regaled with detailed saga of the accident in the mud. Buddy ate fast and kept his round green eyes fixed on the strangers. When the meal was over they stood up without ceremony and went their various ways. Mrs. Bush began to clear the table, scolding Buddy steadily in a low tone. The two men went outside to the other building, and Teddy and Blake followed at a distance, trying to think of something to do that would take them out of the way. It was almost dark by this time: the shadows, that in the daytime looked like pools of ink under the brush, had been diluted and spread and run together over the sand, melting all the brush and the rocks in one dark blanket. They turned together down the valley, walking swiftly on the rough road.

Tramp, tramp, tramp, with a little skipping noise when one of them kicked a pebble. The air was cool and dry and sweet. It grew darker. They passed a tiny fire where two Indians sat on their heels and watched a coffee pot. A long, happy, swinging cry sounded over across the valley, down the mountain. It was dark.

Out of the swelling joy in his breast, Blake cried, "We're out of the States! We're in another world."

Teddy answered with silence. Tramp, tramp, tramp. He loved Teddy and the Navajos and the stars, the heavy yellow stars. For one pure moment things stood still, just like that, and then he knew that it would be one of those moments that would come back some day when there would be least reason to remember. Some instant of time that was waiting for him to catch him some day, perhaps in the middle of a city street in the summer when the asphalt oozed and rose around his heels; out of nowhere, a reasonless ecstasy that wrapped a valley at night, with the Navajos singing, and Teddy.

It hurt. If he could only cry, and spoil it.

Then Teddy caught his breath and said, "Let's not go back to Santa Fé." He felt it too, then. Of course; he had to feel it too. He repeated, "Let's not go back. You mustn't go back to school and I mustn't go on shaking cocktails for hostesses. We'll go to Mexico and get away from everything. How about it?"

Walking swiftly, Blake said, "All right. Yes." It was a perfect thought. He felt no impulse to make plans. Leave it at that; then going will be simple.

"We can drive it easily," Teddy said. "We'll get a car that we can depend on and it'll be simple. I don't care if we never come back, either." He slowed up in his walk, wheeled, and started back to the trading post as though their errand had been finished. Skipping to catch up, Blake followed in step. Tramp, tramp, tramp.

Mexico City, with broad white streets and narrow little slums. There would be fights. He and Teddy would frequent the little cafes ... knives flashing ... the room full of glowering peons allied against them.... He leaped at the swarthy man with the knife who was striking Teddy in the back. The knife felt sharp but not very painful as it reached his heart. Madden was shaking his shoulder and saying, "Blake! My God, he's dying." He stirred, smiled.... Blinking the wetness from his eyes, he blushed in the darkness and shoved his hands into his pockets. Tramp, tramp.

Another flash; sitting in the cheapest seats in the Mexican theatre, surrounded by grimy sweaty people, mustachioed men and mustachioed women. They shouted as the dancer whirled out on the stage, stamping her little red heals. But she looked straight at Teddy, and her eyes were like Gin's, fixed on Teddy in the same mocking, hurt way. And Teddy folded his arms and looked at her with his high little smile, the smile that always made Blake hate him and love him too. The music played; her little heels tapped the stage imperiously. She took the rose from her bosom and tossed it....

But someone was singing; someone really was singing out there in the dark, miles off across the rabbit-brush. Chanting, rising to a hysterical falsetto and swooping down again to a minor note under the one that began the song.... From the shadows back of the store-room another man answered him, for all the world like a coyote.

CHAPTER TEN

Mac drove away and the store was open for business, with the boys hanging about curiously, fingering the stock and getting into Bush's way as he waited on customers. The big cool room was lined with shelves full of folded overalls and canned goods and coloured handkerchiefs and sheepskins and harness and cooking pots and candy. Three or four Navajos, who had been lounging on the door-step when the store was first opened, now lounged on the hay-box and showed no signs either of buying or of going away. When other Indians came in they greeted them, then went on with the business of staring at the stock, or whittling little pieces of wood.

A short fat woman came in with a sack under her arm and two children dragging at her skirt. She plumped the burlap down on the counter and tugged at it until she had uncovered a blanket of a rough weave, which she displayed to Bush's apathetic gaze. He picked up the blanket and looked at it, then put it on the scales and weighed it. After a moment's figuring he named a price, and by her silence she seemed to assent. Blake, chewing cookies, watched her in fascination.

Bush wrote down on a small paper bag, $6.20. Blake read it upside down. The woman looked thoughtfully at the shelves and directed Bush, who put down on the counter a small bag of flour and wrote the price on the bag. After that she went into a deep silence, while the bystanders blinked at the flies and Bush contemplated his toes, chewing gum. She ordered a can of baking-powder and asked how much of the money was left. At the answer she pondered suspiciously, but did not argue. Then she bought ten cents' worth of candy, asked the reckoning again, and left the store with her sack full of supplies, the children trotting at her heels. Bush wrote the transaction down in a big black book and started to rearrange the stock.

Another Navajo rode up on a horse, driving two other horses ahead of him. All three he tied to a post, where they shied at every wandering breeze and kept their noses raised, straining at the ropes. Dusty and cheerful, he strode in and ordered soda-pop and a box of crackers, slamming his money down proudly. He swallowed half the soda at one pull, with his eyes fixed on Blake. "Where you from?" he said.

"Santa Fé," said Blake.

"Yo-to. Good roads?"

"Awful," said Blake. "Terrible from here to Shiprock."

The Indian shook his head. "No, good roads. I came over them yesterday."

"Sure they're good," said Bush. "They're all right, kid. You don't know this country or you wouldn't be complaining about *those* roads."

"They have fine roads at Yo-to," said the Indian. "I was at Yo-to. I was there seven years."

"Where?" Teddy leaned across the counter.

"Yo-to. Santa Fé, that is. I was in the penitentiary for seven years." He seemed very cheerful about it.

"What?" Blake said, in a gasp.

"Yes. I was pretty mad then, but not any more. It is all right now."

He put down the empty soda bottle and bit into a cracker, chatting with his friends in Navajo.

"Why did he go to jail?" Teddy asked Bush.

"I dunno. It was before my time. Probably he helped burn a witch; they always get seven years for that. One of you boys can ride over with me to the well, if you want."

Madden went, and Blake wandered around the house to the back porch, where he was unwillingly drawn into conversation with Mrs. Bush. He had felt awkward with her; she was so silent. But this morning she seemed more talkative. He sat down on the step and listened vaguely, feeling drowsy in the heat. He felt like brooding over the decoration he had found on the wall of his room; a piece of burnt-leather with a picture enameled on it of a ruddy desert mathematically arrayed beneath a setting sun, rays outstretched in all directions. Underneath was a verse burnt in big dancing letters, and he had memorized it:

> Welcome to Arizona
> Where the beauteous cactus grows
> And what was once the desert
> Now is blooming like the rose.

Teddy had been disgusted, horrified, and humourless about it, but there was something — —

"There's a lot of things we don't understand in this world," said Mrs. Bush, and moved the pan in her lap to a more level position to catch the potato-peelings. "I ain't saying that the Mormons are always right, though. I'm not Mormon myself: Mr. Bush is. Anyway, I always think there must be some reason for it all."

"I guess so," said Blake.

"When I was young," she continued, "I laughed at all that, myself. Junior'll go through the same stage, most likely. But I've seen things." She paused and selected another potato. "Mind you, it don't prove anything. But it was queer. It was when I was a girl at home. Mamma and Dad and me had gone to a camp-meeting."

"Camp-meeting?"

"Yes. Not here; I'm from the South originally. Arkansas. We drove over to the meeting-grounds in a wagon and afterwards, coming back, we slept out. It was my idea: I blame myself. It was low country and I should of known better. Mom and Dad were getting along: they were too old to act like that.

"Well, we got back home all right and then we was all sick. Malaria, I guess it was, or typhoid. I've always been as strong as a horse and in a little while I was up and around. But Dad didn't pick up the way he ought to and they took him to hospital. We thought Mom was all right. She just slept all the time." She shook her head and remained silent a moment.

"I didn't worry about Mamma. I ought to of. But I didn't know any better. We were all busy fretting over Dad. Then one night they said he was better and I gave Mom her medicine and went to bed. She told me she felt better too, on account of Dad. I went to bed. I don't excuse myself. There must have been something I could of done.

"Anyway when I woke up it was early morning and Mom was breathing real loud. I called the doctor in a hurry and he came running and took one look and sent her to hospital. He told me not to worry. He said it was a little relapse. I said, 'Yes, but what makes Mamma look so queer?' What it was, she was dying, and I didn't know."

She looked at Blake with wet, horrified eyes, and he waited.

"I went back to bed—I'll never forgive myself, but I wasn't in my right senses yet. The fever kept coming back. I didn't sleep very well, I -*will* say that for myself. Even when I didn't know how bad it was I was worried. I dreamed I was running up the steps of a big building, a funny sort of building I hadn't ever noticed before, and it had big pillars along the front. All the time I was running—I remember it as plain as you are sitting here now——"

And a lot plainer, Blake thought.

"I kept thinking I must hold on to myself and try to expect something nice that was waiting for me in the building. I can't quite say what it was like. As if I was fooling myself in my dream and knew it. I kept running and running and feeling worse."

She picked up another potato, but held it in her hand without beginning to peel it.

"Then they woke me up and said it was morning and time to go to hospital. I went over and hurried right up to her room. And there——" she paused and stared at the henhouse. Then she started again. "There was her bed and the mark of somebody, but she wasn't there. My legs just gave out. I yelled, I guess, and a nurse came and *I* said 'Where is Mamma?' and the nurse said, 'Well, miss, we're crowded so we sent her away.' I said, 'Where to?' Even then I didn't understand. She looked at me queer and said, 'To the morgue.'

"That's how I was told.... Well, I started out and I met my brother Tom, and he said, 'Are you all right, Silvy?'

"I said, 'Yes, I'm all right.'

"He said—he's the sweetest thing in the world, Tom is, if he *is* my brother and

I oughtn't to say it—'You sure you can walk?'

"I said, 'Yes, I can walk. Where's the morgue?'

"So we went over there together, and when I saw it——"

"It was that building with the pillars?" asked Blake.

"The very one," said Mrs. Bush. "And then Dad died too."

She put her hands down among the potato peelings and thought about it for a minute.

"But it worries me, what she must think of me," she said. "If I had only known she was dying. Dying, in front of my eyes, and me not doing anything about it. I wish she'd let me tell her. Lots of times I feel people I used to know around me, listening to me when I'm talking to them. The way you do in your head. But I never have that feeling about her. If she'd only let me tell her."

Blake said, "Oh, she knows."

"How do *you* know?" cried Mrs. Bush, savagely.

CHAPTER ELEVEN

The screen-door slammed once, and Girt looked up hopefully, but decided it was a breeze. She should have known better, for there had been no breeze in Santa Fé for a week. But she was deep in the latest copy of "Screenland" and could spare time only for the paper bag of chocolates next to her.

The door slammed three times, and Teddy called out indignantly, "Anybody home?"

"Teddy!" she squealed joyfully, and jumped up. "I was just wondering when you'd come back. Come in and tell me about it. Where did you go and what happened? You've got a swell sunburn."

He stepped inside and kissed her perfunctorily. "I want some lemonade," he said. "Have you got any? If you haven't I'm going down to the plaza, and I wish you'd tell Blake when he comes——"

"I can make some in a minute," she said. "Sit down and cool off. How did you know I wasn't out of town?"

"Passed by La Fonda and Margaret told me. Where are the cigarettes?"

"On the mantel," she called from the kitchen, and began to chop ice vigorously. "Now tell me about the Navajo country. What happened?"

"Not much. Blake can tell you when he comes: I'm meeting him here. We got home late last night—Mrs. Saville-Sanders wanted to stop overnight in Albuquerque and they were having the Masonic Convention and all the hotels were full. You should have seen her!" He giggled. "She stood up and insisted on having rooms for all of us, and it didn't do the slightest bit of good, naturally. So then she was crushed and wouldn't speak for two hours on the way up, and we were all very tactful and didn't say anything." She could hear him roaming about the room, stopping here and there to pick things up and put them down again. When she came back with a pitcher and glasses, he was staring disgustedly at a small oil painting on the wall.

"Why do you keep that kind of stuff around?" he asked.

"It's Flo, and she said it's worth a lot of money. Here's your lemonade."

"Well, here's to luck."

"Is there any left for me?" Blake came in and sat down, panting from the heat. He held out his hand pleadingly for a glass.

"Did you like it?" Gin asked him. "The Reservation, I mean."

"It was grand," said Teddy. "We took a private jaunt into the country and learned how to trade. We made plans to take out a license and start a post of our own. Oh, but the really important plan...."

"Look here," Blake interrupted, "you're *not* going around talking about that, are you?"

"Gin's safe," Teddy argued.

"She's not. Nobody's safe. Are you trying to ruin it? We promised we weren't going to speak of it at all, to anyone. He's been in town four hours," he added despairingly to Gin, "and everybody has heard all about it!"

"No, they haven't. I swear they haven't, Blake," Teddy said. "Don't get all worked up. I just thought she'd be interested: she's perfectly safe, honestly."

"Go on, Blake," said Gin. "I won't tell. I never tell anything."

Sulkily, he answered, "Well, it isn't very much. We're running away."

She had a sudden pang of fear. "Running away? Where? When?"

"We're not sure about anything: it's all very nebulous," Teddy explained. "That's why we're not telling. It will probably be after Fiesta, just before Blake has to go back to school. We're aiming for Mexico, and of course Mrs. Lennard mustn't have any idea of it. You will be careful, won't you?"

"Certainly I will. But...." She hesitated, her mind struggling against despair. "You make me sick. What'll I do without you?"

"Come along," Teddy said easily. "The more the merrier."

"Madden!" Blake was outraged again. "You don't really take it seriously at all. I don't think you mean to come."

She leaned forward eagerly. "But why can't I come? I'd be useful, really I would. I'd do the cooking for you. I'll try to save up something before we start. Please! Honest, Blake, I'm serious. I am. Couldn't I come? Would it really spoil it all if I came?"

"It's all right with *me*," said Teddy. "Why not, Blake?"

"Because...."

"Oh, you don't want me," she cried. "You *are* afraid I'll spoil it. Let me come. If it looks as if I'll spoil it, I'll take the next train back. But let me try. *Please*. If you don't, I'll get up another expedition by myself, and I'll probably be killed. Go on, Blake. Say yes."

"Oh," he said, relenting, "I guess it doesn't make much difference if we keep it down to three. You're not joking?" He searched her face seriously, and she tried to look as intense as possible. "All right," he decided, "we'll all go. But remember if anyone hears about it it's all off."

"I promise faithfully," she said.

Teddy stood up and reached for his racket. "It's time we're shoving off. Coming along, Gin? You can watch us play."

"Not this trip. Don't you want another round of lemonade to pledge the business?"

"I'm full up," Blake said, and Teddy added, "Better not; we'll splash when we play. Never mind."

"Well then, we'll just shake on it."

They clasped hands and she watched them from the side windows as they drove away. After they were out of sight she stood there, staring at a most uninteresting house across the street and thinking so deeply that she didn't hear Flo come in. "What on earth are you looking at?" Flo said in her ear, and she jumped.

"Are you here already? It must be late."

"No, I'm early. Oh, goody. Lemonade! You're an angel. Did anyone call me?"

"Call? Well, let's see if I can remember...."

"You imbecile," Flo said pleasantly. "Did Russell call?"

"Oh, Russell. Of course he did, constantly, all the time, perpetually. *I* wish you'd tell him to phone the office instead. I get all excited when the phone rings, and it's always Russell for you."

"Why not?" Flo went over to the mirror and started to comb her hair. "Don't you like him?"

"Oh, he's all right, I guess. Are you going to marry him?"

"I don't know. What do you think about it?" She sat down on the couch and put her arms around her knees. "I guess I could if I tried. He's doing pretty well at the office. What do you think?"

Gin said promptly, "Oh, marry him. You said you wanted to be married. I don't know why, but you said so."

"All right. I'll marry him." Flo laughed suddenly and picked up the phone. "I'll tell him now." Just then it rang, and she picked up the receiver. "Hello. Just a minute, I'll see." Covering the transmitter with her hand, she whispered to Gin, "It's for you; it sounds like Harvey. What'll I say?"

"Let me talk to him.... Hello!"

"Hello, Gin. Say, listen...."

"How are you, Harvey?"

"I'm all right. Listen, can't we talk this thing over? I miss you a lot. Let's have dinner tonight."

Suddenly, happily indifferent to all quarrels that had any connection with Santa Fé, she answered, "All right. Come along at six-thirty."

"Well," Flo cried, "When did all this happen?"

"Just now." She handed the phone over. "Now call your Russell." She went into the kitchen and started to clean up, throwing away the lemon-peels. She sang loudly and happily, until her roommate called through the door in protest.

"Sing me a song of a lad that is gone:
Say, could that lad be I?..."

On a sudden impulse, she shouted to Flo, "When you get married would you want this apartment?"

"Me? I'm not really getting married. Did you take me seriously?"

"Oh, I don't know. I thought maybe you'd like to keep it." She emptied a plate into the garbage pail, clattering it cheerfully.

"Russell can't get married yet anyway: he hasn't enough money. Why do you ask? Are you thinking of moving anywhere?"

"Not at all," Gin said, and threw the dish-towel against its hook on the wall. "Not in the *least*."

CHAPTER TWELVE

The car couldn't quite make the hill. Blake shifted gears carelessly, so that they made a terrifying noise and his teeth hurt. Then he settled down again behind the wheel and resumed his gloomy thoughts. The little twists and turns in the road had become second nature to him and nothing interfered with his meditations. He was occupied with a premature regret for a beautiful day which was really just started. For him it was over. He had hurried with his breakfast, very cheerful and making plans in his mind to go right down to the plaza afterwards and see what was going on in town. Probably there would be nothing, but at least he could spend a pleasant morning talking to someone, lounging in front of the Capitol Drug Store and having a Coca-Cola now and then. Besides, who knows? Someone new and exciting might happen along.

Then Mary spoiled it all. He could not blame her as much as he wished, for after all it was simply another morning and she would have been sure to act the same way some other day if she had postponed it this time. It was just one of those conversations. And yet once again he was overwhelmed with that sense of the world outside of him, expecting him to rise up and act in some preposterous worthwhile manner. The world of the adult was perilously close. He hated to be reminded of it.

"Blake darling," she had said, "are you doing anything this morning?" Harmless enough as far as it went. He answered without suspecting anything.

"Nothing special. Can I help you?"

"If you would. I haven't anyone to send up to Sunmount with some flowers I promised to Mrs. Meriwether, because Paul is busy over at the garage overhauling the Packard, and I'll need it this afternoon. I did promise Mrs. Meriwether, and the poor thing's so ill. Could you *possibly*— —"

"Certainly. I'll take them over now, if you like." He stood up and pushed back his chair.

"Wait a minute, dear. It isn't so important that it can't wait a little. I've been waiting for a chance to talk to you."

He hesitated, badly frightened at her tone. Something was going to happen; something unpleasant.

"It's about school."

He sat down again slowly and hopelessly. "I knew it," he said. "What about it?"

"Well.... Here's a letter from the people in California. They're willing to take you for the next year; isn't that nice?"

"No, it isn't." He mused bitterly and added, "How do you know they're willing? They haven't even seen me."

"Well, I pointed out to them that there wasn't much time for preparation. I explained about your last school——"

"Did you have to?" he asked quickly.

"Yes, darling. I was very fair to you, I think. I said that I understood that they had a modern viewpoint, and I said I was sure they'd agree that the preliminary meeting was a formality that wasn't really important. I must say that they sound extremely reasonable. They seem to agree to everything I say. In fact, I'm sure it will turn out very well."

He tried to answer her, but at his expression she laughed. "Oh, darling, don't look so miserable! What a baby you are!"

"Listen," he said desperately. "I've been talking about this place to Phyllis and she says it's terrible."

"Does she? I'm surprised at Phyllis. Her mother said that she was very happy there."

"She doesn't know how terrible it is: she's too dumb. But I could tell from what she said. She says they understand the kids." He spoke in deep loathing.

"Well? Why do you object to that?"

"Oh, what's the use?" he cried.

"Blake! What do you propose to do with yourself if you don't go to school? You can't go on like this."

"Why not?" he asked, without any real hope.

"Besides, when you grow up you won't be satisfied with yourself. You're just a baby, really. I know you don't think of yourself that way, but you are. An ignorant little child. I can't let you grow up without learning any more, can I? How will you ever get into college?"

He answered quickly, "But I keep telling you, I don't want to go to college. I won't go."

"You'll change your mind when the time comes," she said benevolently.

He drew pictures on the tablecloth with a fork, and tried hard to think of what he could say. He would feel his way.

"Listen. Why can't I go away somewhere and have a private education? Lots of people send their sons abroad with tutors. Couldn't you do that? Why can't I go to a foreign country and study languages? If I studied a language I would be learning something. Let me go to Europe or China or——"

"That wouldn't be possible. Not at your age."

"What has my age got to do with it?"

"Darling, I couldn't think of letting you go away alone."

"But if someone should go with me?"

She stood up and gathered her letters. "Let's not argue, dear. *I* wouldn't think of it. You're too young to be that far away from your family; the Ashton boy got into a lot of trouble in Paris and I don't want to see it happen to you. You won't understand: I can't expect you to understand, but you must take my word for it. Hadn't you better get the flowers and go to the sanatorium?"

Now as he left the car in the shade of a cottonwood he reflected that it was a good thing he hadn't told her about Mexico. He had almost said something about it, but she had interrupted. At any rate—he rang the bell at the white stuccoed gate—one thing was certain: he would run away in spite of any objection that Teddy might raise at the last minute. He trusted Teddy to come along if it should get too hot for them in town, but he would need a little managing to crash through promptly. Teddy or no Teddy, however, he must get out of all this or before he knew it he would be on the train with all his text-books packed into the baggage-car. He thought of the new school. A horrible place most likely, with the walls as white as the gate here, whitewashed and lined with dreadful grinning scientific instructors, all understanding him. Understanding him! That was the limit.

He held out the flowers to the assistant and gave the name of his mother's friend.

"She's a little better," the assistant said. "You may see her if you care to."

"No thanks. I—I'm too busy." He hurried out again and climbed into the car. The place always made him nervous, and he could not even remember which of his mother's sick friends was Mrs. Meriwether. He could not face the idea of following a nurse down the corridor to find out. He was afraid of the place; all the quiet little white rooms with windows opening on the green patio. He had spent many hours here and there, sitting on little straight-backed chairs while his mother visited people. Which was Mrs. Meriwether? There was one woman who was thinner every time they came: she always wore pink or blue voile bed-jackets and her hands were skinny and very clean, with shining red fingernails. She kept talking about her fingernails and her lotions and the doctors who were in love with her. Some of the patients were in love with her too, she said. Mary was always very gentle about her afterwards, and never said much on the way home.

Perhaps that was Mrs. Meriwether, or perhaps she was the other one, the jolly one with red hair whose room always smelled sickeningly of ether.

He looked around and found that he had driven all the way down town, and he hadn't intended to take the car down. He started around the plaza, meaning to go back. As he passed the Cathedral he heard an unfamiliar voice calling; it sounded like his name. There it was again—"Blake! Blake!"

He stopped suddenly and the Oklahoma Ford that had been plodding along behind him turned out so sharply that the fenders kissed and made a ringing noise.

"Damn fool!" called the driver from Oklahoma. Blake looked after him nervously and then turned to see who had called. There was a line of cars parked at the kerb, but he could see no one. Exasperated, he backed and looked closely.

"Blake! Here! It was me." A girl leaned from one of the autos, waving at him. He brought the car up next to hers, but could not recognize her. It was very confusing because she undoubtedly knew him very well.

He tried to hide his hesitation. "Oh, hello," he said feebly. "I couldn't see you. How have you been?"

"I'm fine. Where were you going in such a hurry?"

She must know him, but who was she?

"Nowhere. Nowhere special. Would you like to come for a ride?" It was a long shot, but there seemed to be nothing else to do.

She obviously wanted to, but — —

"Do you think I'd better?" She glanced over her shoulder at the church. "I'm waiting for my mother and father. They are at mass. I didn't want to go in and they told me to wait for them."

"I'm sorry." He stepped on the starter, but she said quickly,

"Just a minute. I think it will be all right, just a little ride. You will get me back soon?" Without waiting for an answer she climbed over the side of the battered door and stepped into his car next to him. This activity exposed a good deal of black cotton stocking (*where* had he known her?) and she giggled and jerked her skirt down.

"I don't know if we can go very far," he said doubtfully. "How long will they be in there? Where should we drive?"

"Let's go out to the Albuquerque road. I must be back in ten minutes. It is safer there, because no one will see us."

"Why shouldn't they see us?" he asked wonderingly.

She laughed excitedly and glanced at him with black eyes that looked like kitten's. Where on earth could they have known each other? There was certainly something about her that seemed familiar, but who was she? Had she ever been at the house? Perhaps she had, but if so when? And yet he had a memory that her name was Maria. Certainly, that much he knew—Maria.

"I have not seen you for a long time," she told him. "I think it has been a month."

This was even more mystifying. He answered, "I know, I've been busy."

"So have we," she said. "We have been very busy because Mr. Lyons has started a beautiful big picture. I work very hard with him."

Suddenly he knew. She was the little girl who posed for Tommy Lyons when he did his Mexican murals. Maria Martinez: Mrs. Lyons was very fond of her and treated her like a daughter. He'd been up at Lyons' one day with Mary, trying to prevent her buying a picture from Tommy, and Maria had been posing with a jar on her shoulder. That was all. He was glad that he knew, though.

"How is Teddy?" she was asking. "I never see him any more. I ask Revelita why he is never at home, but she says nothing about him. I cannot make her talk."

"Revelita? Who is that?"

"She works for Meester Stuart. You know—Revelita. Teddy was much in love with her."

"No, he wasn't," said Blake angrily. "You're crazy."

Maria stuck her nose up in the air. "You ask him," she said. "Ask him about Revelita and see how he looks."

Slightly worried, Blake did not argue with her. He had an instinct about it: if he stopped talking about it perhaps he could forget. Maria waited for more conversation, and when it was not forthcoming she changed the subject.

"I see you with Teddy all the time. Every afternoon, nearly, you pass the window when you go to play tennis. I am working every day now in the afternoon. Mr. Lyons is very nice, I think. Mrs. Lyons too, she is a nice lady. She says she will find work for me with the other artists when it is time for them to go away in the fall."

"That would be fine," Blake said absently. Teddy had never even mentioned Revelita.

"But my mother will not let me. Mr. Lyons she says is all right for me to work for, but all the other artists are too young, she says. My mother is very particular."

She paused sadly, and he said, "That's too bad. That's a shame."

"Yes, it is," she sighed. "I must go back to the convent in the fall, she says."

"You too? That's a shame."

"It is silly. My mother thinks that the artists might want me to take off my clothes. She has read about it. I do not want to go back to school."

"I know," he said eagerly. "I know just how you feel."

"I could make so much money by my posing. It is not everyone who can pose. Mrs. Lyons says so. She says I am a good type. What does she mean by that? Does she mean that I am pretty? Blake, you are not listening."

"I am too," he protested. "She means you're strange-looking: your eyes are strange."

"Oh, no! You mean—" her voice was hurt "you mean I am ugly. I know!"

"No, no. You're pretty." He blurted it out, then blushed.

"Oh. Well, my mother thinks that artists are bad and always make love to models. It is not true. Mr. Lyons does not make love to me."

"Of course he doesn't. People don't make love." He hit the railroad tracks with a great bump, and slowed down. "I say, hasn't it been ten minutes?" he asked, uneasily. He hoped that he could go back.

"Not yet surely. Are you afraid? It is nothing to you, is it? Must you go home?"

"No, no." He speeded up again. It didn't matter: he couldn't ask Teddy about it anyway. There must be some mistake. Revelita? No. It was a mistake.

"I think," she said, "that you tell all the girls that you meet that they are pretty. Do you?"

"Me? Of course not."

"I think you do," she said. "I think we are driving too far. Let's stop for a minute and then go back."

"We ought to go back now," he said.

"In a minute. I want to smoke."

"I haven't any cigarettes," he said. "I don't smoke, I'm afraid."

"You are a very nice little boy," said Maria.

"Little? I'm older than you are."

"I think not. I am fifteen."

"I am sixteen," he said loftily. "I think it is time."

"What do you do all day in Santa Fé?" she asked. "Do you play tennis?"

"Most of the time, or ride. This is vacation. What else would I do?"

She sighed and looked at the mountains. "It must be so nice, playing tennis. Don't you have a girl? My brother has a girl. He told me. He comes home so late at night that my father is always angry with him. It is not fair. I must go to bed every night at ten. Sometimes I think it is even better at the convent."

"Are they very strict with you there?" asked Blake.

Her exclamation was an indrawn breath. "It is terrible. It is a prison."

"That must be awful."

"It is terrible. My mother says that they must not know that I pose for artists. I do not think it is bad, but she says they will think that the artists always make love. That is silly: my father would kill anyone who makes love to me. He says so. He would — —"

Suddenly, with no warning at all, she threw her arms around his neck fervently and dropped her head onto his shoulder.

Blake did not move noticeably, but his blood froze and his muscles stiffened. He was petrified with shock. His mind registered a vague scent of hair, black and rather oily. It tickled his cheek. He waited for a long time, hoping that she would release him, but she did not even relax. At last, his resistance broken by waiting, he shifted a little and put an arm around her tentatively. He stopped again and waited to see what it felt like. There was no change in his emotions: he simply noticed that she felt very thin. What could he do? What should he do? He thought of someone coming around the corner, and he grew more and more afraid.

"Oh, Blake," said Maria at last in a high voice, "we are being bad." She lifted her head and he thought that her face looked very odd at close view. She was waiting for something. Oh, yes. He struggled with the conviction that she was waiting for him to kiss her. Would she let go? He kissed her with a sudden little peck at her lips, and she let go.

"You're going to be awfully late," he said.

"Yes, we must go."

He turned the car and started back, going as fast as he dared. He was shaking, and so flustered that he almost ran into a tree. He wanted to get home. He wanted to put her out as soon as possible and get home. Was this what she meant about Revelita? Now he couldn't possibly ask Madden anything about it: some day, perhaps — —

"You're not very fast, are you?" she asked him, breaking the silence for the first time.

"Well, I could go faster, but I'm afraid of the traffic cop," he explained.

"That is not what I mean."

A sudden scream rang out from the sidewalk, and Maria clutched his arm. He pulled on the brake and looked over.

"Maria!" someone was yelling, very stridently. There was a large crowd on the pavement, made of children and a woman. No, there was a little man too, standing behind the woman and pulling feebly at her dress. She was making all the noise, and oddly enough she seemed to be angry at him, at Blake. He blinked and looked at her again.

As he stared, terrified, she came over to the car and jerked Maria out by the arm. She shrieked at him in Spanish, then translated in a louder tone than ever.

"But Mamma...." said Maria, and was forced to stop while Mamma screamed. "Mamma," she wailed at last, "it was all right! It was all right! It was all right!"

The little man approached and tried again to soothe Mamma. She swept him aside and cried to Blake,

"You have taken my little girl riding! She is only fifteen! I will tell the police. I will have you put in jail. I will — —"

"It was all right, Mamma. I tell you we were gone only ten minutes. It was all right."

Maria turned to Blake and added softly, "Go away, quick!"

"Her father will kill you," said Mamma loudly. "He will kill you." She turned and seized the little man by the arm.

Maria stamped her heel in the dust. "Go *away*," she repeated.

Blake went.

CHAPTER THIRTEEN

The unexpected boon of a full afternoon holiday during Fiesta left Gin somewhat embarrassed. She had nothing to do. The afternoon could have been spent sleeping, for she had had little sleep the night before, what with dancing in the streets around a bonfire; but she was too excited to feel sleepy. Time for sleep when Santa Fé had stopped playing and the town had taken off its costume and gaiety; plenty of time for sleep when the carpenters would begin to tear down the platform in the corner of the plaza, and the crepe paper ribbons would hang stretched and faded from the trees. Now the platform was gay with flags and strewn with confetti; last night had been a tango contest before the bonfire-dance, and they were to use it again today for impromptu theatricals—Spanish songs and Indian dances. All the shops were closed today; all the little shopgirls, dressed in skimpy shawls and old family combs, filled the streets to watch the parade. It was Pasatiempo, the day of the Pageant.

Gin strolled through the streets where she could and paused where she must. She watched the parade of the Conquerors; tried to listen to the oration but had to give it up because of inadequate Spanish, and looked on for a long time at the burlesque polo game that the young bloods were playing with burros, spurring the unhappy little beasts towards a huge striped beach ball and catching themselves up on the long mallets. Afterwards she wandered towards the apartment, half planning to bring out her own cherished shawl before the evening, when it was to be worn at the Ball. She thought somewhat of dressing up now, to vie with the others; she wanted to paint her lips and walk around the plaza, round and round, while the boys walked the other way and picked out their maidens for the evening. But she knew that she was tired of standing and weary of the plaza. She would go riding alone and look down at Santa Fé from a mountain top.

She telephoned the stable. Tom was there, but, as he explained, he was leaving to join the celebration.

"I didn't count on no trade today," he explained. "I'm meeting a boy down at the Capitol, but I'll tell you what we can do. I'll leave your saddle in the hay-box in case you come around here: if not there'll be no harm done. You catch yourself a horse. Take oats to 'em—Blanco or the paint will come a-running for oats. Don't let the fence down; just pick your pony."

"Thanks, Tom," she said. "I'll be along."

She changed quickly and walked over to the stable, avoiding the plaza with its crowd. Blanco fell for the oats: she led him out and tied him up while she went for the saddle. It was heavy: she had to rest twice while she carried it back to him. She slung the saddle over his back, cinched it up and then cinched it tighter as he let his breath out, and adjusted the bridle. The street had a more than Sunday quiet as she rode out toward Sunmount: everyone was downtown playing.

Following the trail up Ferdinand, she raced with the shadow of a cloud. There was a long smooth stretch that led up imperceptibly: she ran in the shadow until Blanco looked warm, then she took it easy for a while. The trail grew steeper and led through trees. She stopped to breathe the horse, turning him and looking back. Already they were far up and Santa Fé had begun to mark itself out in squares. She saw autos and trucks hurrying towards the centre of town to be lost among the higher buildings. Under the sun her face felt warm and salty; it was nice to be up here alone.

She pulled the rein: Blanco ducked obediently and started to climb again, stepping carefully in the loose rock. She stopped at intervals that grew shorter as Blanco breathed louder: the horse smell increased and so did the balsam scent. She let the reins fall slack, twisted around the horn of the saddle, while she tied her necktie around her hair to keep it from falling down. The air grew more clear and Blanco's footsteps sounded doggedly musical. It was lovely.

At the really steep part of the ascent she paused and looked at her watch. It was too late to go on: already she had been out an hour and the sun was starting to fall. She knew that sun and how it gained momentum. She dismounted and lay down on the grass, holding Blanco's bridle and looking up at the sky. Long ago the cloud she had raced had won and gone sailing away, but there were more. Their shadows crossed her face and went on. Behind them the sky was a deep blue that had lost its noon ferocity and mellowed. She stirred and rolled her head farther back until Blanco's head appeared grotesquely in the way, calm and cowlike as he munched grass. A dribble of green froth barely missed her head. She rolled away.

"You pig."

Blanco stamped and leaned down for another mouthful, nosing her shoulder out of his way.

"You're a darling," she said idly and comfortably. "Aren't you an old darling?" He blinked a huge eye and went on chewing.

"We've got to go. Do you know that?" she asked. She stood up and looked down at the valley for a moment. It was streaked with yellow; patches of yellow flowers that were much more glaring now in the slanting light, unbleached. The sun was deepening to orange: Santa Fé was almost too small to be noticed except as part of a great scheme of colour. A breeze stirred the pine-branches and lifted her hair-ribbon. It smelled almost salty, as if those misty stretches beyond Jemez were indeed the sea.

"Oh, it's lovely." She threw her arms around Blanco's neck: he was nearer than any tree, and as unprotesting. She slapped him on the flank, climbed up, and dug him in the ribs to start him down the slope, jouncing uncomfortably.

It was quite dark when she trotted into the stable yard. The streets were quiet and lifeless. She tied up the horse and unsaddled him, then turned him into the corral, where he shook himself and walked over to the other side with a dignified, heavy gait. There was a light in the living-room, so she stepped up to the screen door and peered in. Tom was sitting on the cot with his head in his hands, and he didn't look up when she knocked. Somewhat mystified, she called him and he raised his head.

"Come in," he said, as if he did not recognize her.

It was very queer. Her clear sense of health and content evaporated. She stepped in and glanced around, at the bottle on the table and the glass on the floor next to his feet. Usually when Tom drank he grew jovial. Was he sick?

"Have a drink?" he said, dutifully.

"Not now, thanks. Not just before dinner." Unbidden, she sat down in a hide chair and watched him curiously. "Say, what's the matter with you? Don't you feel well?"

"Me? I'm all right." He leaned over and took the bottle by the neck. "I'm all right. I just got some private news, bad news, that's all."

"I'm sorry. Can I help?"

He shook his head. "Somebody's dead."

"Why? Do I know them?"

"No." Holding the glass near the floor, he poured out most of the contents of the bottle. "He was long before your time, Betty."

"It's not Betty," she said. "It's Gin."

"Gin? I beg your pardon. I surely beg your pardon." He added in a dull tone, "Ginny, Wally's dead."

"What?" Her hand went up to her mouth. "Wally? Wally's dead? You're kidding me." He drooped his head again and she jumped up and shook his arm. "Tom! Please answer me. Did you say that Wally was dead?"

"Sure he's dead." He looked at her with red-shot eyes. "He was shot. Them damned Indians in Mexico must a done it. Down at the border: he was missing a couple of days and his horse came home without the saddle. They went out looking and found a Yaqui with his outfit—saddle and gun and all. They couldn't get anything out of him. He claimed he bought it. Wally's dead all right, and buried."

"God." Her eyes filled with tears, mechanical reactions. Inside her head she did not feel ready for tears. She was only shocked and stunned; she was inadequate. "I can't believe it," she said truthfully. "He can't be dead. Why, I knew him!"

"Why not? He had a good outfit and he was American." He slumped down to the cot again and sat in an attitude of maudlin grief, almost theatrical. "Three weeks ago, I gave him hell for leaving Pinto tied by a rope in his mouth. He was always forgetful. I said I'd skin him alive if he did it again while I was anywheres around. Now he's dead and buried."

Gin stood motionless, seeing Wally outlined in clay like the prehistoric skeletons at the Museum. Fragments of coffin strewed the ground around him and he lay stiff, with one arm above his head and his sunken eyes closed and withered. She thought of his arms again. They were huge arms that had often caught her as she jumped off her horse, they smelled of horses and perspiration, and he was fond of a certain checked shirt that he often wore. It was that same shirt that he was wearing now, buried in the clay. No, he would not be wearing his shirt. The checked shirt was in a Yaqui's bundle now, flung into the corner of a hut in Mexico, with a bloody hole in it. Wally was naked and dead and buried. Buried.

Tom had slipped down to the table; his head, clutched in his arms, was sideways on the table and his eyes were closed. Asleep? She poured a drink out for herself and swallowed it. She patted his head.

"You go to sleep," she said. "I'm going home."

It was only after she had walked three blocks that she began to know Wally was dead; dead as everyone was dead that she read about in the newspapers. It was not a new thing, after all. Wally was dead and Mother was dead and Billy the Kid was dead. All of them, all dead and buried. The weight of horror lifted a little and she began to think that she would miss Wally. She could cry in earnest.

She reached the apartment: the door was locked and she had forgotten the key. Sobbing with increasing vigour, she lifted the screen from the front window, raised the sash, and climbed in. She found the sofa in the dark and lay down.

Outside in the street an automobile passed, swishing by the wall. Someone was carrying a Victrola in it and playing a record. She remembered the Ball tonight and sat up, with her head throbbing. What time was it? Had Harvey called before she got home? No, it couldn't be that late. She leaped up and turned on the light. Eight o'clock, and the room was in a mess of cigarette stubs and clothes flung over all the chairs. Flo must have put on her costume in a hurry.

The 'phone suddenly began to ring, and she picked it up.

"Gin?" It was Harvey. "I've been calling for hours: they said at the office you were in town all afternoon. Where've you been?"

"Oh, I went riding."

"Well, gosh, I thought you'd run out on me. Are you ready?"

"Listen, Harvey, I can't go." She paused, then repeated, "I can't."

"What? Why not? Are you sick? You sound sick. What— —"

"No, but something terrible has happened."

"What is it?"

"Wally's dead."

"Who's dead?"

"Wally, down at the stable."

"Oh, that's a darned shame. That's too bad. What killed him?"

"The Indians."

"*What?* Come off!"

"No, the Mexican Indians. Yaquis or something. They shot him for his horse and saddle, and he's dead."

"That's certainly a darned shame. I don't think I ever knew him, but — —Well, why can't you come out tonight, anyway?"

"Why, Harvey. I can't. Don't you see? I can't go."

"No, I don't see." He sounded very irritated. "You mean because this cowboy is dead? What's that got to do with you? Were you crazy about this bird?"

"No, but...." she hesitated. It was hard to express. "Don't you see, he's dead and buried and all that. I can't go on a party. I knew him. I used to go riding with him, and now he's— —"

"Say," he said flatly, "I don't see that at all. You're just worked up over nothing. You're alone down there, aren't you?"

"Ye-es." Her voice was uncertain.

"Now I tell you what you'd better do. You wash your face and get ready and I'll be right down, as soon as I get dressed. I've got to shave. Is there anything to drink down there?"

"I don't know." She spoke humbly. She was beginning to feel very foolish and useless.

"Well, you fix a drink and take it. That'll help you. You've just got the blues, that's all. It's a shame he's dead, but you better take a drink. I'll be back as soon as I can."

He was very comforting, but she wished that he hadn't called just then. She looked dolefully into the bathroom mirror, at her swollen streaked face. Why did she always have to act so dramatic? She rubbed cold cream into her cheeks and felt the tank. There was enough hot water for a bath.

Harvey came before she was ready and she shouted through the door that he must come in and wait. When she came out, wrapped in a bathrobe, he was standing at the window with his pipe in his mouth, looking masculine.

"I'm sorry I was so cuckoo," she murmured, sincerely.

"That's all right. I brought something over." He waved towards the couch, on which there were parcels—sandwiches and candy and a bunch of red roses.

"Oh, Harvey: you're a darling. I've been so nasty to you."

She made him eat some chocolate and put a rose in his buttonhole. He was not in costume, except that he had wrapped a red sash around his waist.

"Now you make me feel that I'd better not get dressed up," she said. "We'd look funny all different."

"No, you go ahead. These affairs are given for the girls anyway. Go on: I'll wait."

She dressed in the kitchen—bouffant black skirt and purple fringed shawl, with a high comb and a mantilla. He was pleased with her when she came out.

"You look swell," he said. "Regular Señorita. Give us a kiss."

She held up her face.

"That's the kid," he said. "Not sore at me any more?"

"No, You've been awfully sweet."

They drove over to the theatre and although it was half an hour late, nothing had started. A crowd of costumed people were in the lobby. Gin paused at the door and looked around for Flo. She was over in the corner with Russell and a party of friends.

"Wait a minute," she told Harvey. "I've got to talk to Flo."

Holding her roses carefully, she wedged a way through the crowd to Russell and plucked at her roommate's arm.

Russell turned and greeted her. "Golly, who's your beau?" he asked. "Flo, look at the flowers."

Gin pulled Flo off a little way. "I've been dying to find you," she said. What was it she had to tell? Then she remembered Wally. Even now, soon as it was after the catastrophe, she was shamedly conscious of a sort of pleasant anticipation, the prospect of causing a sensation with her news, the expression that she could foresee on Flo's brightly interested face.

"I heard about something this afternoon," she went on. Again she was swamped by the calamity and carried out of herself. The truth of it hit her again, as it had on the road home.

Dead and buried. She pictured to herself his closed eyes and the clay.

She stopped smiling. The corners of her mouth dulled and her eyes grew wide.

"You know Wally...."

CHAPTER FOURTEEN

"Teddy! Teddy!" The call had sounded so often that to Teddy himself his name had undergone that strange transformation where it had become a senseless word, without end or meaning. He was sick of it. If he heard it once more, he told himself, he would smash something—preferably the stage scenery. One prop pulled out and there would be a splendid crash.

But he had no time to waste, pulling props or contemplating ruin. He was hurrying as fast as he could. He stacked a heap of gossamer costume on a rickety chair, started off in answer to a plaintive cry, and then rushed back just in time to keep the costume from tumbling down. "Teddy! Come here a minute." There was no time to say "please," no time for anyone to adopt the usual pretence that they were asking him and not ordering. He put the costume down again, more firmly, and tore off in the direction of the ladies' dressing-room. Mrs. Saville-Sanders wanted to be pinned up.

"Teddy!" That was Bob, at the other end of the stage. "I need some help here."

"Teddy! What in hell did you do with that foundation cream?"

"Teddy! Come and fix my eyebrows. I look like a ruin. What's the matter?"

"Teddy Madden, come and tell me where to put this jar. You stand out there and look. Do you think so? No, I'm sure you're wrong...."

"Ted, Gwen Saville-Sanders wants you to fix the flower that goes in her hair. Hurry up, for God's sake. She's on a rampage."

He dashed into the dressing-room again and Phyllis Parker snatched up a wrapper and screamed. Startled, he paused and glanced at her. Her legs were long and bare beneath the wrapper: she clutched it to her flat bosom like Diana surprised in the bath, and glared at him.

"Oh, don't be such a damn fool!" he snarled, overwhelmed by the imbecility of it. "D'you think I have *time*...."

"Teddy! Teddee.. ee.. ee." A maliciously long-drawn wail that set his teeth on edge. He was dripping with sweat and his face was smeared with dust and plaster. For a quarter of an hour the audience had been clapping spasmodically, now someone had started them off on a slow, ominous, steady applause that beat on his ears terrifyingly. Well, what if they did get tired and go home? Of course they wouldn't, but what if they did? He would be glad. He wanted more than anything in the world to go into a corner and sleep; if anyone called him he would show his teeth like a rat. One more idiot yelling for him....

The stage director came in and held up his hand, spreading an area of quiet through the crowd until it reached the outer corners.

"Silence! Silence! please. Everyone *must* be more quiet. I was out in the back, the very back, and I could hear you all the way out there. Please be more careful, even if you are excited. Now then, is everyone ready? Are all the props in place? Madden, have you looked it all over? All right then. I'm going to give the signal.... Curtain!"

In the hush behind the scenes following the creaking of the curtain, Teddy escaped and crept out into the audience through the side door. He wiped his face and tried to relax, refusing to look about him, even at the stage, until he should have regained his temper. The affair was well under way when he allowed himself to look.

Well, it seemed to be going without too much of a hitch. It was impossible to follow it closely after so many rehearsals. Unless someone made a new error, he wouldn't even notice the customary little slips that they were so used to. He was fogged, worn out. His head drooped to one side and he began to breathe with a dangerous regularity, then caught himself up and straightened his back. The trouble was that he had not had a drink all day. He had promised Mrs. Saville-Sanders to see to it that no one was drunk at the opening of the Vaudeville, and in the face of careful taboo, how could he have managed to take anything for himself? No, it was better this way. But now it was safe: as soon as he had a chance he'd get something. No one would be able to last through the Ball without a little help. His head slumped down again.

Through the uncomfortable doze he heard the long-drawn clapping that meant the end of the first act. He sat up quickly as the lights went on. They'd be needing him. He went back to the stage door, stopping with Billy Trewartha, who was in charge of the curtain.

"Got a drink?" he asked. It was an unnecessary question, since he had stopped Billy twice from taking nips before the show started. Billy harboured no grudge, however. He took a flask out and mounted guard while Teddy did his best to repair his nerves.

The second act was launched and he went back to his old seat. The audience was taking it pretty well. Of course the people in front would like it because it was a family affair, but these chaps didn't have to applaud unless they meant it. The broad comedy went over much better than the highbrow offerings. Natural enough, he reflected; it was really much better. He craned his neck and took one glimpse of the front rows, then sat back, satisfied with their carefully appreciative expressions.

Next act started off awkwardly, some mix-up with the lights to begin with, and a lot of frantic flashing—yellow and red and blue, each new colour greeted with irreverent applause. The curtain went up before it should have, too. Perhaps Billy had finished the flask too soon. Oh well, it was not too bad. The light was fixed at last as it should be; a single red beam at the corner of the stage. Then Phil Ray stepped into it and walked slowly, or rather danced—for his step was controlled and deliberate—to the centre. His arm was raised, covering his eyes, and he crouched as he walked. In the centre of the stage he stopped, turned slowly in a series of notes from the music, and paused again. The playing was louder, working up to a crescendo. He dropped his arms, stretched them down along his sides, then flung them back and stood with his chest high, his ribs sharply serrated, his neck ridged with shadow as his head fell back. The shaded half of his body looked purple in the red light, shining from an angle. He was naked.

There was a stir, a gathering disturbance in the audience. Suddenly the rustling and whispering concentrated in the centre of the second row. In the darkness Teddy thought he saw a great moving shadow. What could it be? Someone was talking, forgetting to whisper. Someone was arguing. An usher opened the door into the lobby and held it; someone was going out. The electric light streamed in from the back, near Teddy, and illuminated the majestic form of Mrs. Montgomery Pearson, walking out of the door. She walked like a sacred elephant, and her jet necklace swung back and forth across her armoured bosom. She moved slowly, with upheld nose but downcast eyes, into the pure air of the outer night; after her, blinking a little and stooping more than usual beneath the horrid burden of so many astounded stares, Mr. Montgomery Pearson followed with her shawl.

The door swung shut behind them and the house was in darkness again. Only the red light persisted, shining on the imperturbable Phil, who went on dancing. Teddy managed to get backstage just as the act ended.

Back there they were not taking it as humorously as he had expected. Phil came off the stage in a fit of hysteria and everyone was comforting him. The place was in a mess: everyone was indulging in the luxury of indignation, and Teddy leaped into the middle of it until the stage-manager extricated him and sent him forth to calm down the performers. Bob was the most militant: he was all for sending the Pearsons out of town by official order from the Mayor.

"I can see the humour of it as quickly as anyone can, my dear boy," he explained to Teddy, "but damn it, we must protect the colony. What's to happen to free speech and all that if we allow the bigots to criticize us?"

"I'll start circulating a petition tomorrow," said Gwen. "Teddy, remind me of it in the morning."

"Teddy," said the stage-manager, "see if you can't make the property men get down to work. I promised the undertaker that he can have the chairs back in time for a bridge party tomorrow."

"That reminds me," Mrs. Saville-Sanders said, "that I want to talk to you when you have a moment to spare, Teddy."

Phil plucked at his arm and asked him feebly if it would be wise to bring action for libel. Bob thought that it would, and walked off with him, saying, "I'll give you the address of my attorney in Albuquerque."

"Before I forget," Mrs. Saville-Sanders persisted, "I want to ask you to be sure to come to my bridge on the eleventh, Teddy. Don't forget, will you? I shall count on you. And I wanted to say that you've been a dear boy and a great help tonight. I don't know what we should have done without you." She turned to Bob, who had come back. "That's a nice boy," she added.

His heart bounded in triumph. The accolade at last!

"Teddy! Come here a minute, will you? Someone has got to help me pack up the costumes."

He ran gaily to obey the last order of the evening. All was well. His face was as the face of Wellington after Waterloo.

CHAPTER FIFTEEN

At the door of the Gymnasium, Blake halted suddenly, peered around the room, and swore under his breath. Hearing his own whispering voice was a comfort to him, but it did not dispel his panic. It was embarrassing, torturing, to be so early at the Ball. Anyone seeing him would think that he was eager. He could not bear to be eager, or to be thought so. No one had come but the orchestra and a few town people who had not gone to the Vaudeville. Had they seen him? He withdrew to the darkness outside and plucked nervously at the elastic that held the tall sombrero on his head. If anyone should see him now they would think that he was being kept waiting by someone. Irresolutely he turned and went to his car, to sit there, he told himself grimly, until he had counted twenty people going in to fill up that appalling room.

How had he happened to be so early? He wondered what he was missing, and had a spasm of jealousy. Now he was sorry that he had dashed so quickly after the show. He had been so afraid that Mary would ask him to take Phyllis or Lucy over to the Gymnasium. He had wanted to start this evening of festival all alone and unhampered. He had gone for a short drive, the Circle Drive up towards Taos, and had been confident he would be late. Probably they were still at the theatre, talking about the Pearson business.

He crouched there smoking until he had counted his twenty people. He decided to count ten more before risking an entrance. At twenty-seven he saw Teddy coming with a crowd, showing the tickets of the party and carrying coats to be checked and in general being very useful. If Teddy had come, it would be safe. Blake stood up and went into the Gym. The orchestra had begun to play listlessly, saving its energy for later. Teddy greeted him impatiently.

"Where were you? I lost everybody," he said. "I just picked this crowd up. Gwen and the others went tooting off and I thought you'd be with them. Where's your mother? None of them are here. What's the idea?"

Blake explained that his mother had gone with Mrs. Saville-Sanders for an extempore committee meeting. "I heard them say they'd have some coffee and get the important business over with right away. I ran away. It's probably awfully dull. I wouldn't worry about it."

Teddy tried to thrust his hands into his pockets, but his velvet trousers had no pockets. "It's very queer," he said. "Why didn't they ask me too? I had a lot of things to say; I must say it's queer. Do you think it means anything?"

Blake thought he understood. "I hate to miss things, too," he said. "It isn't anything, though. You weren't on the committee, that's all."

"I suppose that's why." Teddy looked at the door. "Here they are now, anyway. Whatever it was, it didn't take long."

The room had filled and the officials of the party had begun to line people up for the Grand March. Mary, loitering behind with the matrons, tried to persuade Blake to go in, but he resisted her.

"You go in, if you want to," he suggested. "I haven't any partner; I don't want to go. You walk with Madden. He wants to march."

They walked off arm in arm and he climbed to a bench and stood perched on high, to see more clearly. It was very colourful and pleasant; the Gymnasium did not look exactly like a palace, but it didn't look at all like a schoolroom. In the centre, the marchers were lined up and the orchestra began to play "La Cucha-racha." They marked time, moved, started off, and he saw them one by one as they passed. Some of the costumes were beautiful. Many of them had no appreciable connection with the period of the Conquistadores, but no one cared about that. The girls, at least, were faithful to their conceptions of Spain. There were short-skirted women with flat black hats, and long-skirted girls very bouffant and draped with lacy shawls. There were women with mantillas and women who had had to tie their high combs to their heads with silver ribbons or elastics, to hold them on in spite of their Eton crops. Some women had dressed for evening and then had relented enough to put roses in their hair. The men were armoured knights and cowboys and trappers and Indians. All sorts of Indians. Some were dressed in costumer's leather and buckskin and some were last-minute affairs of plain shirts with tails out, and moccasins. Phil Ray had rebelled at the indeterminate Indian tendency: in reaction he was wearing a slouch cap and checked trousers from one of his dance costumes, and if anyone asked him why, he retorted, "I'm an Apache."

Everyone—men and women—had taken advantage of the Carnival to do what they wanted to do in the matter of paint. Boys were languishing and red-lipped, with fierce cork mustaches and Vandykes and heavy hairy eyebrows. Girls' cheeks flamed orange and scarlet. As the room grew warmer, everyone began to streak slightly.

Three times they marched round the room until Blake was heartily tired of "La Cucha-racha." So was someone else. A determined young man stepped from the march and went up to whisper into the ear of the orchestra leader. The signal was given, the tune changed at last, and the line melted into a dance. Blake remembered his duty and climbed down to claim Mary until the first intermission after the dance. Afterwards he went back to the line of wall-flowers to watch the others. He was standing behind a line of old women who had "just come to look on," and listened to what they were saying while he kept his eyes fixed on the dancers. They were amusing, but horrible. They were so spiteful and helpless. The worst of it was that they all agreed; if one of them said something they all nodded and added to the statement. They agreed on the prettiest costume; they nodded in concert if one of them ventured a view on the morals of some unfortunate girl who danced by.

During the third dance, well on towards midnight, he plucked up courage enough to leave the faded ladies and claim Gin for a dance. She was in high spirits. He had watched her from across the floor; now that she was in his arms breathing in his face he understood better why she was so excited. Corn liquor, probably. They went twice around the room without speaking.

"Are you having a good time?" she asked him then. "You look glum."

"Not very. Does anyone?"

"Oh I do," she said. "I love crowds, don't you? Everybody in the world is here. Even from Taos. It's simply marvelous. Have you seen Phil? Isn't he rare?"

He glanced at her obliquely and decided that she was pretending. No one could be enjoying it, really. Everyone was trying too hard, as they always did in crowds. He was depressed. Merry-making always seemed to leave him out. Was it his own fault? Of course the wags were busy, being clownish. Clowns were always too busy to think about enjoyment itself. Why couldn't he be like that? If he could even stop thinking about himself it would be more comfortable, but he couldn't. No one ever could. Mary couldn't, or Teddy.

The dance was ended; she took his arm and started to lead him from the room.

"Where are we going?" he asked suspiciously.

"Out to the car. I want a drink, don't you? Harvey's waiting."

"No. If you don't mind, I won't come along." He was afraid of Harvey; afraid that he would be in the way. Harvey had danced with Gin held very close, in a very proprietary manner.

She tugged at him. "Come along. You don't have to drink if you don't want to, but please come on. Please. I hate sitting out there alone with him."

That settled it and he stopped short. "No," he said flatly. "No I won't."

She cried out impatiently and began to argue, as he knew she would. But whatever she was saying, he did not hear; he was suddenly listening to another voice behind him, that struck him with terror.

"There's Blake Lennard," he heard, and knew it was Maria. "Oh Blake! turn around."

He obeyed, but he was very fearful. Maria was hanging to the arm of Mrs. Lyons, and she was dressed magnificently in a Spanish dress of black lace. Inherited, probably. She narrowed her eyes as she smiled and he thought nervously that she looked like the—was it basilisk or obelisk? Mrs. Lyons, always stupid, now beamed at them maternally as Maria seized his free arm. Maria ignored Gin completely. "Aren't you going to dance with me?" she asked him.

"Surely. See you later—just a minute." He pulled away and hurried out, with Gin looking back wonderingly at the little girl.

"Good heavens. Who is that little vamp? What's been going on between you?" She was giggling.

"Where's the car?" he asked impatiently. "I'd better stay a while."

Harvey, when they found him packed down in the back seat of his auto, was very jovial, and if he objected to Blake's presence he at least gave no indication of it. He was very insistent upon sharing his bottle.

Blake still held out. "I don't like the taste, really."

"He's got to keep his wits about him tonight," Gin explained, and patted his shoulder affectionately. "Don't you make him take anything if he doesn't want to. He's saving himself for a little girl back there who's waiting for a dance. You ought to see her, and the way she looks at him!" She laughed heartily. "Blake's been carrying on behind our backs, that's what the trouble is. Carrying on!"

"Oh, stop it. Do you really think I ought to go back and dance?"

"Ought to? How do I know what you've been doing with her? You won't get home alive if you don't, if that's what you mean."

He sighed unhappily. "Give me a drink," he asked pleadingly, and Harvey shouted with laughter.

He pounded Blake on the back as he handed him the little cup. "That's the boy. He's all right, he is. *I* used to think Blake was just a sissy, but he's all right. One of the boys."

"Of course he's all right," said Gin. "I always told you he was. Now he's turned out to be John Gilbert besides."

"Stop giggling!" Blake flushed with rage. "You're always giggling."

She giggled again. Harvey put his arm around her and she made no effort to push him away. In spite of himself, Blake had to look at them. He couldn't make up his mind what to do. If he started to go they would object, and insist on his staying. If he went back to the ballroom he would have to dance with Maria; he couldn't face it. He sat still, being miserable. He tried to keep his eyes off the shadow that was Gin and Harvey, twined in each other's arms, but there was no help for it. In the corridor made by the tonneaus of the cars, lined up in three straight rows, other people were pouring drinks and sitting close together. He heard the sounds; whisperings and laughter and soft chinking. Any evening at the Country Club it was the same. Why did they come all the way to Santa Fé to do it? He thought again—and again and again—of that hint Maria had given him about Teddy and Revelita. Teddy too? He could not believe it. Teddy, who painted so well and talked so well and was so impatient of all this; just as impatient as he himself had been. Teddy never mentioned it. Would he never understand the rest of the people in the world? Was there nothing for it but to go on alone, travelling by himself through life? He looked disgustedly at Gin, just as she came to a late realization of his mood, and pulled herself away from Harvey.

"Where's Teddy?" she asked, as casually as if she were continuing a conversation. "I want him. Harvey, go on and get him: you're falling asleep."

Harvey stirred and shook his head. "I don't want to. I'm sleepy."

"Oh, don't be mean. Go and get him. I want to tell him something."

"I'll get him," said Blake. He leaped out, disregarding her protests, and went back to the ballroom, forgetting all about Maria until he reached the door. Then, in a panic, he hid behind a tall girl who was going in, and looked around fearfully before he started over to Teddy in the corner. Janie Peabody seized him as he walked by her. He was surprised, because Janie never noticed him any more than he noticed her. Now she was very cordial. She insisted on making him sit next to her, holding his arm and talking very seriously and incoherently. He knew that she was drunk. He remembered that it was one of the things the old ladies said when they sat against the wall at parties; Janie drinks too much. That Peabody girl ought to have more sense. If someone would persuade her to go to a sanatorium — so sad at her age.... He wondered how to get away, but he couldn't think fast enough. She wanted to dance.

Unhappily, he pulled her to her feet and started around the room. It was unutterably difficult. He couldn't listen properly to the music, and she was unsteady and leaned heavily on him. When she began to sing he looked at the floor, and this naturally led to many collisions. He looked up again, desperately, and just then Janie decided that she was tired and slumped to the floor. She sat there, laughing.

"This isn't happening," he thought frantically. "It's a dream."

He persuaded her to stand up again, pulling her by the wrists, and tried to lead her to the side of the room. Just then he caught a glimpse of Mary, white-faced, looking the other way. He had thought that he could not be more miserable, but when he saw her he reached the limit of his endurance. He handed Janie over to Trewartha, and then took a deep breath and walked across the floor to Mary.

"I was looking for you," he said, abruptly.

She bowed her head. What was she going to say to him?

"You look tired," he added. "Would you like to go home? It's pretty late."

"Thank you, Blake," she said coldly. "I don't think that I want you to come with me."

"Why not?" He suddenly thought he understood. "You don't want me to come home any more?"

"Oh, don't be dramatic. Go away, please. Don't stop enjoying yourself."

His anger with Janie burst out now. "You're the one who's being dramatic. Very well, I won't come home."

"That's your own affair." She opened her fan and started to wave it delicately. "Mother...."

"Blake, please. We'll talk about it in the morning."

He muttered, "No we won't," and started away, feeling decidedly ill with passion. On his way to the door he blundered into Mrs. Lyons, who stopped him.

"So you're leaving us?" She smiled down at him with her customary indiscriminate fondness for youth.

He managed to collect his manners, saying politely, "It's a nice party, but I'm sleepy."

"I didn't mean tonight," she explained. "Wednesday I mean. I understand you're really leaving on Wednesday. Such a shame, when you're having a good time! My boys hate to go back to school."

His jaw dropped as if someone had hit him on the back of the head. "Wednesday?"

"Did I misunderstand?" she said. "I'm sure your mother said Wednesday." "Oh, of course. Yes, Wednesday. Well, I must be going. Good-night."

But that was in four days! He walked towards Teddy, instinctively seeking help. Why hadn't she told him? She had been too excited, probably; she had forgotten or put it off until she would have more time to argue. He rallied in his despair, and grew calm.

"Teddy," he said, over Lucy's shoulder, "I've got to talk to you."

"Shhh." Teddy waved him to silence. Bob was talking to Lucy Parker, and he wanted to listen.

"It's a modern orgy," he was saying. "It's the nearest approach to a public orgy that we'll ever have in New Mexico."

Lucy glanced around, with her lips pursed scornfully, and remarked that for an orgy it was very dull indeed. "Look, there's hardly anyone here to perform. Everyone is being either very dull or most circumspect."

"Of course," said Bob triumphantly. "That's the modern note. All the essence of the orgy is in the aftermath. We've lost the knack for public vice. We've— —"

"Oh, for Pete's sake," whispered Blake, "come on. This is awfully important."

"What is it?" They strolled off.

"I'm in a mess. I just found out—Oh, Lord." He had caught sight of Maria coming towards him. "Come on outside. I'll never be able to tell you in here. It's terrible."

They stepped out of the door and were almost knocked over by Gin, who was in a whirl of dishevelled shawl and escaping hair. She flung herself upon them.

"Thank goodness you're here," she cried. "Take me home. I'm in the most awful mess."

"Another?" asked Teddy. "Well, tell us all about it."

They went to Blake's car and crowded into the front seat.

Teddy nodded to Gin. "Well, tell yours first."

"I couldn't possibly tell you," she said. "It's too involved. It's indecent besides. Just get me out of here before Harvey finds me, because he's in a state and if I see him again I'll pull his hair out." She laughed in a shrill voice. "The old sheep," she said hysterically. "He acts exactly like a sheep."

"Well, then, wait a minute. Blake's really in trouble."

"Oh." She calmed down immediately. "I'm sorry. Is it serious?"

Blake sat tragically slumped, with his chin propped on his hands over the steering-wheel. "I just heard that Mother's shipping me off on Wednesday," he said.

The others gasped in chorus.

"Wednesday!" cried Gin. "You mean to school? California? But that's just four days from now!"

"Three days. Today is tomorrow. I mean it's three o'clock."

In the silence the music in the Gymnasium sounded foolish and far away. Someone scuffled and laughed in one of the nearby automobiles. "You can't argue with your mother?" Gin asked.

"No. She's in a state about something. I can't even talk to her decently."

Teddy said, "Wait till morning. Maybe she'll be all right then."

"No, I don't dare risk it. It wouldn't do any good. I'll just have to go unless I get away before she catches me."

They must have understood him, for they remained silent. A little breeze came from the mountains.

Gin took a quick, noisy breath and cried, "Well, why shouldn't you? Let's all go away now. This minute, while we have a chance."

Teddy said nothing. They looked at him imploringly, waiting, but he did not say anything. At last Gin took him by the shoulders and shook him.

"You're not going to back out, are you?" she begged. "You want to go away, don't you? You said you did. Come on. Blake, you tell him."

Blake couldn't speak. "Oh, all right," said Gin petulantly. "Neither of you mean it. Come on, Blake, let's get out and leave him here. He can stay in this old town till he rots. I'm going to Mexico."

Blake's mind seemed to burn up in a quick ecstatic thought of it. He shuddered.

Teddy spoke at last. "Of course I'm going. Don't be an ass. I'm just thinking." He sat still, and then said, "First we'd better get coats. Give me the checks. It's going to be cold."

"Oh," Gin cried impatiently, "we don't need coats. Come on."

"Wait a minute. Give me the check, you lunatic." She handed it to him; he took Blake's and went to the door. When he came back with the coats——"There," he said. "We don't have to be quite half cocked, do we? Now about money. We'll need gas, Gin: try to snap out of it. I'm broke. Is everyone?"

"No," said Blake, "I've got fifteen dollars."

"I cashed my salary today," said Gin. "I have twenty. That's enough, isn't it?"

"It's got to be. All right, let's go. Let's see where we can be by morning." He wrapped his coat around him and sat back.

Blake laughed loudly. "Ready?" he called. "Everybody ready?"

"Let's go!"

The engine raced for a minute. Blake backed the car, then started down the road to Albuquerque.

CHAPTER SIXTEEN

Before they had come to the gap that cuts a sharp high line of hills and marks the half-way point to Albuquerque, the sun came up. It was gloriously melodramatic over the little crawling black car; it spouted red and orange over the sky, and the fresh midsummer wind was cool and ethereal. Gin held up her chin and closed her eyes for a second, sniffing. Then she opened them hastily, for she was driving and it would not do to go to sleep. Not that she felt sleepy; she was still tingling and wide-awake. She peered into the mirror at Blake, asleep and white-faced in the tonneau, and wondered at his indifference. But the poor kid had been through a rotten night: only in the last half-hour he had stopped jerking and looking back over his shoulder at the empty black road behind them. It was awful to be a kid. Even the law wouldn't help.

Thinking of the law, she felt afraid again. It was time to ask Teddy the question she had thought of hours before, but had put out of her mind.

"Teddy," she said in a low voice. He woke from his doze, beside her, and cocked an eyebrow. "Teddy, are we all right with Blake?"

"Why not?" His voice was husky: a morning voice.

"Couldn't we get into trouble driving off with the car like this?"

"No. It's his car. His own car."

"I don't mean robbery; I mean the Mann act, or kidnapping, or whatever you call it. He's a minor, isn't he?"

She watched him and grew more uneasy, for worry appeared on his face.

"Gosh," he murmured. "I don't know anything about the law.... You think they might send the police after us?"

She shrugged helplessly. He pondered for a minute, then turned around and tugged at Blake's foot.

"Wake up, kid—you can sleep again in a minute. Listen; how worried do you think your mother will be?"

Blake sat up with a guilty jerk and rubbed his eyes. He was frightened at first; then he remembered and smiled. Watching him through the driving mirror, Gin knew that she would fight for him no matter what the police did. She'd keep him out of school if he didn't want to go back. She'd take care of him.

"What did you say?"

"We were wondering about your mother," said Teddy. "Will she send the police after us? You're a runaway, you know."

The air was growing lighter, changing to pink. Blake looked around him at the passing juniper-bushes and said slowly, "She won't think I've gone. Not till this afternoon. I said I wouldn't be coming home; she'll think I went with you."

"But when she finds out?"

"I'll tell her myself. I'll telegraph something, and then I think she'll be too proud to send after me. Don't you worry; I'm not worried. Isn't this great? Isn't it? Let me drive awhile."

"We're going to wash as soon as we reach the river," Gin said flatly, "colds or no colds."

The sun was high when they came to the bridge and they took turns bathing, hidden more or less from the highway by a bush. Afterwards they had coffee in Albuquerque and sent a telegram to Mary: "GONE TO MEXICO HEALTHY WRITING DO NOT WORRY LOVE BLAKE."

"There," said Blake, "that looks perfectly reasonable. Now she won't worry."

Teddy drove out of town, while Gin sat in the back and watched him, wondering what he was thinking about it all. Was he enjoying it, or was he beginning to be sorry? His face reflected in the mirror was impassive and close-lipped. She stared at it until her eyes closed under the brightening sun, and she slept.

They stopped at last in a field and lay down in their coats on the ground to sleep, surrounded by stumpy bits of yellow grass growing in the dry soil. Gin dreamed that she was back at her desk in the office in Indiana, typing. A long complicated dream it was, with a dreary wretched atmosphere about it. It was even worse than the real thing had been. She woke in a bad mood; the relief that flooded through her when she found herself lying in a field with her shoulder dented by a rock couldn't dispel the eerie horror of it. She looked at her watch: it was only noon. Shifting quietly, she lifted the edge of her coat and put it over her head to keep the sun from giving her more bad dreams. A burro was grazing a few yards away. He raised his head as she raised hers, and they looked at each other for some seconds with similar expressions of sun-drenched drowsiness. He sighed and dropped his head to the grass again. Vaguely comforted, she lay down and went to sleep.

They got up at four, because they had seen signs advertising a rodeo at Magdalena. This meant going forty miles out of the road to El Paso, but as Blake pointed out, they had the rest of their lives ahead of them. They drove into town at eight o'clock, when the whole place in the ordinary course of events would be going to bed. Tonight, however, it was different: the dusty streets were trampled with thousands of hoof-marks and people swarmed along the side of the road. Cowboys in blue jeans crowded the stores and leaned against the doors, picking their teeth. Four or five cars were parked on the main street, and in front of the post office a group of Indians sat on the ground, waiting for excitement.

Gin was too stirred to sit quietly. She stood up in the seat as they drove slowly down the road, turning her head this way and that. "It's so *thrilling*," she said.

She looked at Teddy and impatiently shoved his shoulder. "Isn't it thrilling?" she repeated.

"Let's find something to eat," he answered. There was a slight argument over this. Gin and Blake wanted to cook their own food, and Teddy was in too much of a hurry. In defence of himself, he developed a plan. He found out where the hotel was, and after making his companions promise not to say anything, he bargained with the proprietor for jobs for the lot of them. Gin, he protested, was a professional waitress and he and Blake were expert dishwashers. The man consented to take them on for the next two days, during the rush, at wages of ten dollars among the three of them, and meals included. Teddy tried to get rooms too, but this was no good. The proprietor compromised by selling them three blankets for fifty cents apiece. Afterwards they ate bowls of chili con carne and drank coffee and condensed milk, then drove out of town to make camp.

Rolled up in her blanket, Gin was almost comfortable. It was romantic and satisfactory under the chilly stars. Once, towards morning, she woke with a jerk and noticed that the world seemed much too large and quiet. She sighed and tried to edge nearer to Blake. The air smelled of sage and horses: she wondered dreamily why she was there, and then she remembered and was happy before she went to sleep again.

Breakfast and lunch next day merged in the kitchen into one long period of torture—aching arms and weary feet for Gin, and greasy, coolish water for Teddy and Blake. She carried trays back and forth from the dining-room and the flies followed everywhere. But the meals were good enough and they would need the money. After lunch, when they had rested and felt more cheerful, they brushed themselves off and went to see the most important part of the rodeo, the bronco-busting. All three of them had seen rodeos, the big famous ones that went even to New York and London, but this one was different and more fun. The horses were really wild, and lots of them were new to the game. The men were not professional riders, but cow-hands who spent most of the year working on ranches.

Gin and Blake and Teddy had never seen anything like it. The riding was thrilling. They stood on tiptoe to watch over the heads of the people who were so unlike the sightseers at Vegas on the Fourth of July. Town people, the Mexicans who lived in Magdalena and Datil and Socorro and San Antonio, were mixed up with the ranchers' families who cheered their own punchers or watched excitedly silent when they had bet on the length of time some man would stay on the back of his horse, watched eagerly while he was tossed and bounced and jerked by his bronco.

There was a race of wild mules; the animals were saddled for the first time in their lives and the riders had to run them in a straight course for the goal. One of the mules got there: the other three rid themselves of their riders and then dashed round and round, kicking up wildly and almost splitting themselves in fright at the dangling stirrups and straps. They were caught and set free in a corral.

The air was dusty and hot. After two hours of it, Gin had had enough. She retired to the car and sat down there, waiting until the boys should want to go home.

She sat with her back to the field and tried not to think at all. The only way to get anywhere, she knew, was to be an absolute imbecile, never reflecting on the past or the future. For instance, if she should start to worry about the trouble she had caused at the couriers' headquarters, or if she had any qualms about leaving Flo and Harvey, she would weaken. Instead, she stretched out in the sun and began to recite the multiplication table.

The boys came back in a great hurry, having looked at the time and remembered their duties at the hotel. For the next three hours Gin forgot everything but her legs and arms: the dining-room was jammed. There was to be a big party at the dance hall and the boys wanted to go. When she tried to stay behind to rest, Blake begged her to come for only an hour, and she gave in. It wasn't that she was so tired really, she confessed.

"I look like a mess," she said to herself. But she borrowed a knife from the kitchen and trimmed the fringe of her shawl, and they all polished each others' shoes as well as they could. They were an hour late for the beginning of the dance.

The orchestra was pretty bad, of course, and the floor was rough. Gin danced once with each of the boys and then suggested that they mix with the others. They ran off thankfully and left her alone, but it was not long before a tall cow-hand requested the honor of the next number, and after that she was so busy that she had no time to be tired.

The music seemed to get better. She danced often with a stocky man who had a scar on his chin and was a better dancer than he looked. He was foreman at a ranch, in for the celebration, and every now and then he disappeared and came back smelling of whisky. She would have liked a drink, but civilization had not yet reached Magdalena and no one offered her anything.

Another man told her that he was home-steading. She said, "But aren't all the good lands used up? I thought — —"

"Yes, ma'am. My land ain't so good. I'm thinking of starting a sort of store when it's settled, and making out that way. The only thing is, a fellow gets lonesome and there aren't enough girls. I've known boys to ride eight miles both ways, just to call on a girl." He surveyed her morosely. "If you was thinking of locating out here, you wouldn't have much trouble getting yourself a husband. Take me, why, I've been looking for a wife for a couple of years. Can you cook? I seen you stepping pretty lively with the plates, up at the hotel."

It was at that point that she called Teddy and reminded him that they had not danced lately. She apologized afterwards, but he said it was just as well she had done it while he was still winner at the crap-game.

It was late and cold when they went back to camp, but they were in good spirits and hummed all the way. After Gin had cuddled down in her blanket she could not go to sleep. She listened to the blood pounding through her lips, and thought of Teddy and Blake so near her, and wondered if anyone had ever been happier.

CHAPTER SEVENTEEN

It was six o'clock in the evening. Blake stopped with his arms full of all the wood he had picked up, rabbit-brush roots and twigs and a few bigger branches hacked unscientifically from half-dead trees. He wanted to stay out here a minute, on the other side of the hill from the fire. Gin was busy cutting up onions, probably, and if he got back there before Teddy did she would make him help. Anyway, there was no hurry for the wood: the car was full of bits that they had picked up all day. There was wood and a water can and a saucepan and there were two loaves of bread and an assortment of knives and forks from the Magdalena hotel. In a few minutes it would be his job to pull it all out, but not yet.

He could see smoke from the fire hovering in the air. Probably she was mixing the stew now. He thought pleasurably of that stew, potatoes and onions and corned beef, most likely. Still, he would stand here until they called him. He loved them both, but it was good to be alone. How alone he was, even with that smoke so near him! He sighed with content and looked in the opposite direction, at the place where the sun had just sunk out of sight. The land was perfectly flat. A few bushes and cholla plants stood out like giants on the plain. It was hours' since they had passed a fence; just land and land and land, with here and there a side road.

Two days now until they reached Mexico; two days at the most. He could hardly believe it. He looked up at the sky and wondered what would happen to them. Where would they be in ten years? Still in Mexico, still together? He hoped so. The rule of the expedition was that no one should think of anything but the present. Teddy had made it; he had said, "Let's not remember anything or plan for anything. Let's just go along." Now Blake broke the rule; he wondered how they were acting at that moment in Santa Fé, without him. Mary would be dining with Bob, perhaps, and talking about him. Probably she was being very offhand and modern. He could hear her saying, "He'll be back before the week is out. I know Blake. He'll do his sulking and then come back perfectly cheerful." Oh, he said defiantly to himself, will I?

It occurred to him then that he had really heard her saying it. Had some part of him been back there, waiting in the air and listening to Mary? When he said "Will I?" perhaps she had jumped a little, thinking of him saying it just at the time that he did. He followed the idea. Perhaps even though he was standing here on the desert, there was a part or shell of him in that room where he had been, telegraphing.

He felt very clear about it, and willing to go on with the speculation. His mind worked better these days. Every mile he went away from school seemed to help.

He was almost ready to form a theory that one learned better if one was happy; perhaps in Mexico he might even become interested in algebra.

"Yoo-hoo!" Gin was calling him. "Stew-hoo!" He picked up one last twig and went back to the fire, smiling. Teddy was measuring out coffee-grounds to put in the boiling water, and Gin told Blake to cut the bread. They started to eat as fast as they could, though the food was still almost too hot.

All of them were wind-burned and peeling, with dry lips from the dust and the sun. They looked bigger, somehow, than they had been when they started out. And yet it had been only four—no, five days, Blake said aloud, since they rode out of Albuquerque. No one answered him, and for a while there was no noise but tin spoons on tin plates.

"Ho-ho," said Teddy, sighing, and stretching out his legs. "I ate too much." They settled back comfortably, their heads pillowed on rolled blankets. It was getting dark enough to show up a few pale stars.

Gin said, "You're all wrong about not mentioning Santa Fé. It's the best part of being out here, thinking about town and how nice it is that we're not back there. I keep wondering how Flo is getting along with the dudes, and then I look around and feel great."

"That's the way it is with me," said Blake. "I want to think about it all the time. The old plaza and all that. How do you think it turned out with Phil and the Pearsons?"

"Oh, I bet nothing happened at all. Nothing ever happens there. You always think it will, but it doesn't. Something else will turn up pretty soon that they'll be talking about instead of Phil."

"They're talking about *us* now," said Teddy, in a tone of deep satisfaction.

There was silence again. Then Blake hit the ground with his fist. "I feel so *great*," he said.

"We all do," said Teddy quietly. To Blake, still in that queer state where everything was crystal clear, it came suddenly that he would never forget any of this moment; the orange-glowing fire or the two pastel-shadowed figures sitting beside it. Teddy's profile, with turned-up nose and ruffled hair, was lowered to the branch he held in his hand, poking the ashes at his feet. He would always remember that, and the smell of burning cedar.

Gin sighed. "If it starts raining again tonight I'll go to sleep sitting right up in the car. I felt lousy last night."

"Oh, it won't rain tonight," Blake promised easily. "The sky is clear." It was his trip and he felt responsible for nature. The fire burned down to a useful small smouldering size while the night crept up around them.

"It's queer how easy it is not to worry out here," Gin said. "I used to worry all the time about everything, and now nothing seems to be very important."

"I know," said Teddy.

"You? You never bothered your head about anything," she said resentfully. "Money or anything. I used to be so jealous that I could have choked you sometimes."

"What do you know about it? I did too worry. I didn't say anything about it, that's all."

Blake listened carefully to this strange talk, and now he felt impelled to break in.

"I don't understand either of you. Why should you have worried about anything? You're grown up. If I ever get to be twenty-one, there won't be another thing in my life that I can't manage. Just to think that no one will be able to tell me what to do, after that! You don't know when you're well off."

"Oh, yeah?" Gin pushed a charred log farther into the fire. "Well, wait until you get there and you'll see how easy it is."

"People waste too much time. Always talking about little things that don't make any difference anyway, and fussing around with people they don't like very much. They ought to stop doing what they don't want to do, if it doesn't make any difference to anyone. They ought to go and do what they really want."

"What do *you* want to do?" asked Gin. "What things really do matter? You act as if there were something else to *do*."

"I don't know. It depends on who you are. Teddy really wants to paint; it really matters to him. What do you really want to do?"

"I don't know. I want to have a good time in Mexico, that's all, and it looks as if I'll get it." She patted Blake's hand and smiled at him.

"Well, if you're satisfied now it's just because there isn't anyone else around to give you ideas," said Teddy suddenly. "We're in an artificial state just now, the way people always are when they travel. When we get some place in Mexico and start getting acquainted with people, things will be complicated again for all of us."

"I can't understand you," Blake repeated sincerely. "I used to think that everyone knew all about things, everyone but me. I always felt like saying to older people, 'Here, what about life? What is it like?' I honestly thought they'd be able to tell me. Now I'm getting there myself, and I know that I have as much sense as anybody, but it isn't much."

He put his hands behind his head and looked at the sky and was happy, in spite of the ignorance of humanity.

"We ought really to have some ready-made answer to questions about life and all that," said Teddy. "We all fool around and fool around trying to figure out an answer, and at the end we just take what we have."

"We take what we have and then we quit," Gin said gloomily.

"Whatever we have. It isn't any better than what other people have, that's the tragedy of it. It's no nearer the real truth."

"What truth?" asked Blake. "Is there one?"

"Oh, yes." Gin sounded shocked. "There's got to be truth. Why, here we are, all alive. What's it all about, if there's not some truth?"

"It's just an accident that we're here. Look at us and then look at all this space. Why should we have been picked out, especially?"

"I don't say that we are, especially. I don't mean just us, just the three of us or even the whole race. I mean the world and the universe and so forth. Why does it keep on going?"

"It doesn't have to have a personal manager," Blake insisted. "It all runs by system. Science."

"Sure. All right. But what's the system? Truth, of course."

"Call it God while you're at it," drawled Teddy, who was almost asleep. "That's what you're working around to, anyway. 'Some call it Evolution'...."

"I don't mean Evolution," said Gin scornfully. "Now you've got me all mixed up. I'm talking about the truth, that's all. Things *are* true. If I didn't think so, I'd commit suicide. I wouldn't even take the trouble to commit suicide, I'd just stop living."

"Well then, by all means go on believing in truth," said Teddy placidly.

"It isn't believing," she insisted. "It *is* so."

"I never feel like committing suicide," said Blake thoughtfully. "It might hurt."

"Well, that proves it," Gin said triumphantly. "You have a standard."

"No, I haven't. That doesn't follow." He stood up and stretched,

Teddy said, "Of course you have. You believe in painting, don't you? Some of it is better than the rest, isn't it? Well then, you have standards."

"Oh, no. Those are personal preferences. What I am, not what I think. My likes and dislikes aren't my thoughts."

"How can you decide which is you, and which is what you think?"

Blake was silent. It was too much like that old thing that used to puzzle him so at breakfast; the picture of the girl on the box of cornflakes. She held another box of cornflakes on her lap, with a picture on it of a girl holding a box of cornflakes, with a picture of a girl.... Once upon a time he had studied that picture until he was nearly crazy, trying to imagine what happened after the boxes had become so small that he couldn't see them. He grunted and rolled over with his nose burrowed into the blanket.

"That's why we bother our heads about little things," said Gin. "When we try to figure out big ones, we go crazy."

"Some people do," Teddy said. "They stop thinking about everything but that one question, What is Truth? Scientists...."

"I know," she said impatiently. "Arrowsmith stuff. What difference does it all make?" She unrolled her blanket and started to take off her shoes.

"We're like a legend," Blake said after a moment. "Three brave people going out into the world. It makes me feel brave to sleep next to a fire. I don't know why."

"It is like that," Gin said eagerly. "Like the Three Musketeers, but there were four Musketeers really, weren't there? I always forget. Perhaps we'll pick up a fourth somewhere."

"I hope not," said Teddy. "Four would be too many and we'd have trouble."

"I don't see why."

"If we pick up another man, he'll start making love to you; and if we pick up another girl one of us will start making love to her."

"I don't think so." Blake sat up. "We don't make love now, so why should anyone else start us off? We're different."

"Oh, you think so?" Teddy laughed in a nasty patronizing manner that disturbed Blake. "Wait a while. We know each other too well, this crowd. Take it from me, someone else will spoil it."

Blake was uneasy. He hated to carry the conversation farther, but he was too worried to let it drop. "Why should we change?" he persisted. "We get along."

"How do you know? How do you know Gin gets along, for instance? Or that I do?"

Gin interrupted, saying, "Oh, shut up, Teddy. Never mind," she added to Blake, "he's talking through his hat. Go to sleep."

Wonderingly, Blake looked from one to the other of his companions. They were glaring at each other.

"Leave him alone," said Gin.

"Why should I? What are you trying to do; mother him? This is no nursery." Teddy lay down with his back to the others.

"Well then, try to act your age," she retorted, but there was no answer.

In the next few minutes the quiet of the prairie was disturbed by Teddy's soft snores. The atmosphere had cleared and everything was peaceful. Blake sighed and flopped over in his cocoon.

"Gin," he whispered experimentally.

She lifted her head. "I can't sleep." They peered at Teddy, and she added, "I think I'll take a walk. It's awfully early. Do you want to come along?"

Softly he untangled his feet and put his shoes on again; she did the same. They tiptoed away to the road and set out at a good stride. The starlight was blue.

"I kept thinking of poetry," he explained, "and I couldn't get to sleep. It kept going round and round in my head."

"What poetry?"

"Just little pieces that I've read. I thought this one over and over:

> "While waves far off in a pale rose twilight
> Crash on a white sand shore.

"I don't think it's right, but that's the way I remember it."

"There's just one poem I remember," she said. "You know— —

> "From too much love of living,
> From hope and fear set free....

"Do you like that one too?" he asked. Incredible! They stared at each other.

The light of a ranch house was ahead of them, and they paused.

"Let's go back," she said. He nodded and they turned.

"Listen, Gin," he said thoughtfully, "I know what Madden meant when you got sore at him. You don't have to worry about me. I know what he meant."

"Of course you do."

"Only I don't like to talk about it, that's all. I just don't like it and I won't talk about it. You see? I don't want you to think...."

"Of course I see. Never mind."

"I don't want you or Madden to think I'm dumb, or...."

"I don't think you're dumb at all."

They turned up the field again towards the fire.

"Gin," he asked, "do you think that any other three people ever had a better time?"

"That's what I was wondering. I don't see how they could, the way most of them live."

He sighed. "I wonder if we'll go on feeling like this. Sometimes I'm afraid."

"Afraid of what? Of course lots of things could happen. We might have an accident, or perhaps...."

"That isn't what I mean. I'm not sure what I do mean. But—well, if one of us should die it would be terrible, but that isn't the most dangerous thing."

"What is it, then?" She was whispering now, standing near the fire. Teddy was still snoring.

"People change so. You might change, Gin. Even I...."

She shook her head and he thought that she looked very sad. "I'm grown up," she said. "I'm more grown up than you are, and I know about myself. You're the one who will change, or Teddy. I don't want to go back; I don't want to do anything but this."

He believed her, and felt lighter. "Don't worry about me. I don't want anything else either. Look at the star up there, over that tree. It's green, isn't it?"

Teddy tossed a little, and mumbled.

"We'd better be quiet," whispered Gin. "Go on back to sleep."

CHAPTER EIGHTEEN

Teddy woke up very early in the morning. The sun had come up and had lost its colour: it hung above the flat line of earth like a colourless lantern, a lamp made of gold but with no light in it. He did not know what had waked him, but there was a chattering birdlike noise from a hummock nearby. Prairie dogs, and they had been making a terrific row, probably. One of them put his nose out of the hole as Teddy lay on his side with wide-open eyes, watching. He crept out slowly, his plump little body elongated with caution. He drew up his back legs one after the other very gently, and sat down on the top with his paws dangling before him. His head turned slowly and he looked at the world with squirrel-like eyes that saw no importance in anything, even in the three prone giants around the smoking pile of ashes. Then he suddenly started to run close to the ground, looking for something to eat. Teddy sat up, and he squeaked and rushed down his hole again; his tail gave a last little twitch as it disappeared.

Gin's head was covered with her blanket against mosquitos and dew; there was nothing visible of Gin but a wisp of hair. Blake's face was turned to the sun, and his mouth was open. They both slept deeply. It must be very early indeed.

Teddy yawned, rubbed his eyes and shook his head. He propped his elbows on his knees, and his chin on his fists, waiting for something to happen. The day was gathering colour again, as if light from the sun were slowly filling the air, mixing imperceptibly, sinking down from the layer of sunshine above the clouds in little driblets, like a mixture of drinks. The ground had dropped away from under the sun. Beyond the long shallow swell of ground in front of him there came a ghost of a yell. Teddy leaned back among the folds of the blanket, and watched until he saw far off the silhouette of a man on horseback driving before him a flock of sheep, almost invisible in the irregular ground.

He moved nervously and looked again at Gin and Blake. He was depressed, full of a foreboding and a loneliness. Every morning when he woke he was uneasy until he had spoken to the others, and he was never completely at his ease until they had stopped at a store or a gasoline station and chatted with the attendant. It was like a feeling of guilt, the conviction that came to him every morning that he had no right out here under the sky. He was trespassing. Surely some day he would be waked by a policeman, and ordered out of the desert. There must be a law about sleeping out like this. One night he had been so uneasy that he had waited until the others were asleep and then crept back to the curtained car to sleep under some sort of cover, at least. It was all right unless he woke up at night: if he slept straight through and found himself still there in the morning, with no enemy standing beside him, he felt triumphant and safe for the day. Just now he was nervous. That man with the sheep—would he see them and come over to order them off? It was ridiculous, of course. The land didn't belong to the shepherd any more than to himself, or Gin.

He looked at the sky. There were no clouds, and it would be a hot day. Where were they going? Would they be in El Paso today? He twisted around and looked at the tires of the car—no flats. The corner of the packing-box where they kept the groceries was sticking up above the door. He put on his shoes and stood up quietly.

When Gin and Blake woke they found him tearing a branch into bits, feeding the small beginnings of a fire.

"What's the idea?" Gin asked crossly. "It's too early to get up."

"I was cold," he answered calmly, and put one foot on the branch while he jerked at it.

"Cold! It's so hot that we'll be getting sunstroke."

"Well then, get up. The coffee will be ready soon."

They protested, but they helped him with the breakfast. It was growing really hot and they were glad to get into the shade of the car. Blake poured some of the water into the radiator and watched anxiously as it disappeared.

"We're using a lot of water," he said. "I hope we don't run out."

"Not yet," said Teddy. "There'll be a couple of stations before we get to town. Climb in."

The morning was dull and dusty. They passed one or two ranch-houses and rode through miles of flat lime country, and Teddy's depression grew stronger. He felt as if he had forgotten something. What was it? But of course he had forgotten something; he had forgotten everything. Everything in the world was back in Santa Fé or Minnesota. Did it matter? He was starting out afresh, without anything in the world but himself. They were all doing it. It was a rebirth. He looked around at the desolate country and wondered what the Garden of Eden had looked like. Blake and Gin were silent and impassive, strangers. He was so miserable that he was afraid he would start to cry, and their firm young faces were cruelly indifferent.

He knew what he wanted. He missed breakfast in Santa Fé, in the Eagle Cafe. He wanted to go in and sit on a stool before the counter, the greasy crumb-strewed coffee-splashed table that stretched the length of the restaurant. He wanted another breakfast with the *Capital Times* to read; a stale roll and coffee with milk in it, and people to talk to. People! And afterwards to stroll down De Vargas Avenue to the barber-shop, or to sit in the taxi-stand and have a smoke with Harvey, waiting for trade. He wanted to talk to someone, Harvey or the barber or the Mexican who lived next door and kept a goat in the back yard.

And the others—Bob, or Lucy, or even Phyllis Parker. Who was new in town, he wondered? Who was being taken for the Circle Drive, or eating lunch in the

Plaza?

The car stopped in front of a little frame shack with a green door and a red gas pump. A Mexican came out when Blake honked the horn, and filled the tank sullenly. Blake tried to find out something about the road ahead. How far was El Paso? Would there be a place where they could have lunch? Did the Mexican have an extra carrier for gasoline? The man grunted in reply. He had no gas tank. El Paso wasn't beyond three hours' drive. A place for lunch three miles farther on. Road pretty good. He shuffled back into the house and slammed the door.

There was a poster on the wall that looked new enough to be contemporary. Curiously, Blake sauntered over to examine it and to read it aloud:

"Prize Fight," he said. "Between José Baca and the Montero Kid. Tonight. Seats twenty-five cents. Reserved fifty. At the Palace Theatre...."

"Where is it?" Gin asked eagerly. "I'd like to see one. Or is it over?"

"It was last night, I guess. September sixth — what is today? Is it the seventh?"

"It doesn't matter," Gin said. "Come seven, come eleven.... Isn't it my turn to drive?"

They rearranged themselves and settled down. Teddy was in a daze. There was something he had forgotten; he had certainly forgotten something. Gin had reminded him of it. What was it?

The morning passed slowly and the sun grew hotter. Blake was excited, more and more so as they drew near the border.

"What do you think the border looks like?" he asked cheerfully. "I expect a sort of chicken-wire fence with flags on each side."

"I think it'll be a row of milestone things," Gin said. "We can tell better when we hear them talk. Blake, you wink at me when you hear someone say 'Carramba!' and we'll know that we've arrived."

They screamed with laughter. Teddy stared at the road and frowned. Come seven, come eleven. What was it? Something was wrong: he had forgotten something.

"I'm off to my love with a boxing glove," sang Blake. "Whoops!"

His voice irritated Teddy. It was too shrill, too young, too joyous. And Gin too: Gin was a sentimental fool. Why need they talk? Couldn't they ever be quiet? What was that thing he had forgotten? It was important, too; very important. What was it, and what had it to do with a prize-fight? He shook his head violently, trying to jog it.

They had lunch in a little fly-swarmed town. He worked his way through two pieces of leathery pie, trying to eat himself back to good humour. They teased him about his appetite and his irritation almost broke through. On the way to the car Blake swung himself over the door and it was all Teddy could do to keep from striking him in the face.

He was tired of the car and the kids; he didn't want to sleep out of doors any more; he was worried about what they would do in Mexico. And there was something he had forgotten.

He was driving. All of a sudden it happened. For the first time in his life, something came over him that was so powerful, so cleanly sweeping, that he was utterly without strength before it: he was wax.

He remembered.

September seventh, September eleventh. Mrs. Saville-Sanders. The bridge party. It was September seventh today, and on the eleventh Mrs. Saville-Sanders was having a bridge party, and she had asked him to come and help.

He squeezed his eyes together and looked at Blake, sitting next to him, and then he turned around wonderingly and peered at Gin in the back seat. All three of them were dusty tramps, sitting in a dusty car a few miles from El Paso, miles from Santa Fé. How perfectly appalling. How had it happened? It was a bad dream and he couldn't wake up. Seven from eleven left four—four days to get back. Four days to climb out of this pit.

Blake was kneeling and looking back at the road. They had passed a sign. "Gin!" he cried, and his voice cracked with rapture. "Only eight miles!"

Teddy slowed down, stopped, backed the car up and started the other way. Back to Santa Fé and Mrs. Saville-Sanders. Out of the haze, the receding mist, he heard a tiny babble of voices pleading with him, but they meant nothing. He did not listen.

"What's the matter? Where are you going? What is it?"

Then Blake understood, and there was an anguished shriek. "Madden!"

An incredulous, outraged cry.

He stepped on the accelerator and his blood flowed faster as he felt the road slipping by. Mexico was safely behind him. He was waking up. Who were these people? He stepped on the gas.

They fell quiet behind him. Blake had crawled over the seat and was sitting with Gin, whispering with her. Teddy glanced at them in the mirror, sitting with their heads together, and closed his mouth grimly, clenching his teeth.

It would be four days. Four days to drive with two sulking children, and then he would be back in Santa Fé, safe. If he drove steadily it would be shorter, maybe: three days if he had any luck. Three days if he averaged twenty-five miles an hour. Only three days.

CHAPTER NINETEEN

On the back seat Blake crouched next to Gin and tried to think. He looked out at the road, the same old road repeating itself, and tried to know what to do. The wind blowing by his ears frightened him. He was terrified of the stranger in the front seat. Things were happening too fast; he could scarcely catch his breath.

Couldn't he get Gin to help?

He looked at her hopefully. He knew now that they must leave Teddy: the madman in the front seat must be overpowered and left behind. He was a traitor. The best of the adventure would be gone, with only two of them left. It was hard, but it was not fatal. They could do it. He looked at her, waiting for help....

Her eyes were fixed despairingly on Teddy's back, and she looked more miserable than Blake himself, and as hopeless. He stared at her, and he knew that he was alone. Something had taken the strength out of her.

He was alone.

He shrank back into his corner, bouncing as the car bounced. Something was happening to his face.

With a last spurt of defiance he flung up his arm to shield himself.

THE END.

Lector House believes that a society develops through a two-fold approach of continuous learning and adaptation, which is derived from the study of classic literary works spread across the historic timeline of literature records. Therefore, we aim at reviving, repairing and redeveloping all those inaccessible or damaged but historically as well as culturally important literature across subjects so that the future generations may have an opportunity to study and learn from past works to embark upon a journey of creating a better future.

This book is a result of an effort made by Lector House towards making a contribution to the preservation and repair of original ancient works which might hold historical significance to the approach of continuous learning across subjects.

HAPPY READING & LEARNING!

LECTOR HOUSE LLP
E-MAIL: lectorpublishing@gmail.com